AMBER ARGYLE

WINTER'S HEIR

FAIRY QUEENS 7

To Chantry, Adam, and Zach,
Nobody mention this to them and let's see if they ever notice.

Copyright © 2016 by Amber Argyle
http://www.amberargyle.com

First Edition: May 2016
Library of Congress Cataloging-in-Publication Data
LCCN: 2016907685

Argyle, Amber
Winter's Heir (Fairy Queens Series) – 1st ed
ISBN-13: 978-0-9857394-9-2

TO RECEIVE AMBER ARGYLE'S STARTER LIBRARY FOR FREE,
SIMPLY TELL HER WHERE TO SEND IT:
http://eepurl.com/l8fl1

OUTSHINE
THE
DARKNESS.

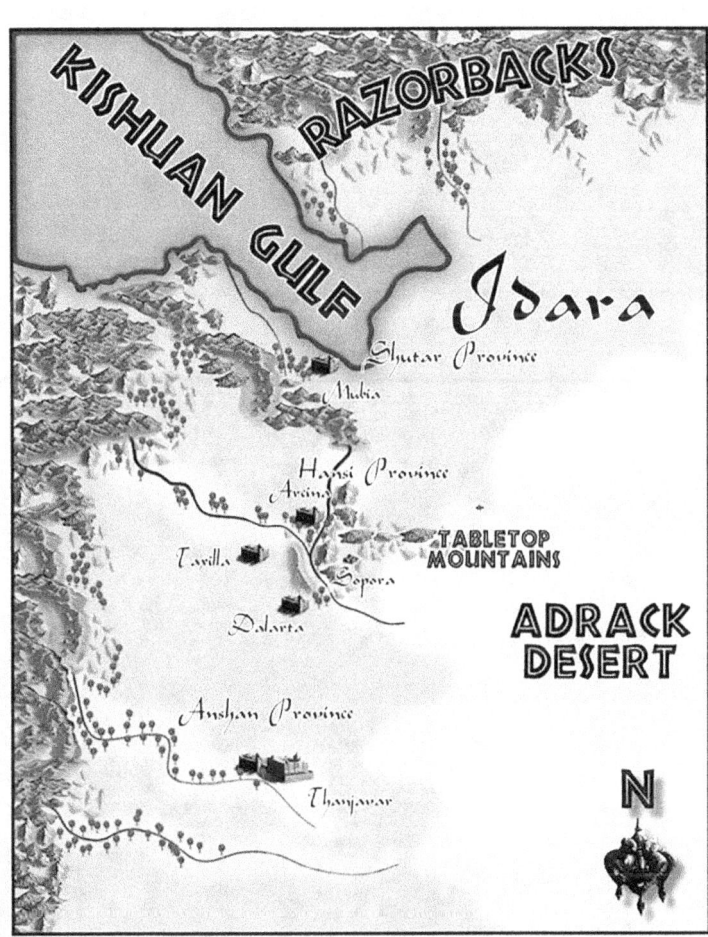

B eneath the threatening gray sky, the wind seemed to be holding its breath, only letting out little strangled gasps every now and then. Gasps filled with the bitter tang of winter. Adar had left the Winter Queendom behind, but apparently, it wasn't done with him yet. Cheeks stinging with cold, he wiped his dripping nose and scanned the ground for something, anything, he could use to make a fire.

"You're never going to find anything dry enough to burn," Sakari chided from where she and Elice lay, belly down before a small body of water. In the clear depths, fish swam back and forth, taunting Adar's growling stomach.

He scratched at the itchy layer of mud on his exposed skin—a protection from the swarms of mosquitoes—and said, "You just worry about getting us something to eat."

Feeling another bite at his cheek, he slapped at the mosquito. Then he turned away, pried up some moss, and started making a pile. He was going to build a fire, the smokiest fire he could, to keep these blasted mosquitoes away. And to work some warmth into his frozen hands. He could ask Elice to draw the cold away with her magic, but every time she touched him, he felt the wrongness of what he had done. What he was *still* doing.

"If only I had some line and hooks," Sakari groaned.

Adar glanced over at Elice, who was staring into the water as if mesmerized by the fluid movements of the fish. Adar and Sakari were covered from head to toe in sealskins to ward off the chill, but because of her magic, the cold never touched Elice. She wore only a clannish overdress and underdress that had once been fit for the princess she was, but it was tattered now. Even her shoes were long gone, lost to the river. As he stared at her dirty bare feet, an image of Tikaani's knowing face as he'd slipped under the freezing, rushing river flashed in his mind. That horror had compounded when Elice had dove in after him. He shivered from more than just the cold, wondering if the winter queen would ever really let them go, or if she was just biding her time before attacking them again.

"I've never seen so many fish, or so big," Elice said, wonder in her voice.

"These are tiny," Sakari huffed. "At my grandparents' village, the fish are the size of toddlers."

Elice seemed to consider for a moment. "You're teasing."

"I am not!" Sakari said with a laugh. "All summer long, the salmon charge up the river to spawn."

Even Adar had a hard time believing that. Elice pushed her hand into the water. A moment later, fish encased in ice began to float to the surface.

Sakari blinked. "And how exactly are we going to get them?" Elice pushed to her feet and waded into the frigid water. Her dress lifted, revealing shapely ankles and legs. Adar was powerless to look away.

"Showoff," the other girl muttered.

Elice threw a grin over her shoulder then promptly lost her balance and fell in. Dripping mud, she came sputtering back up. Adar and Sakari took one look at her and laughed. Adar promptly inhaled a lungful of mosquitoes. Choking and gagging, he spit while the girls laughed even harder. Elice started choking too.

Sakari had been smart enough to cover her mouth with her shirt. Elice's hand shot out and a wave of sharp cold slammed against Adar. The mosquitoes dropped dead, their high-pitched whining abruptly cutting off.

In the silence, Sakari let her shirt fall from her mouth and stared at Elice. "Sometimes you scare me."

Adar was just relieved to have a reprieve from the insects' attack. Now if only the clouds would go away and the sun would come back.

Elice grunted as she surveyed the dead insects littering the water around her, carnage that the remaining fish were happily taking advantage of. "The cold wasn't as strong as it should have been." She frowned and started tossing the dozen or so ice-encased fish back to Sakari.

Adar put his back to the girls and lit the moss on fire, making sure it would burn long and slow. The relief at being so close to the flames again nearly made him dizzy.

Sakari suddenly stood over him, staring at the fire. "How did you get it to burn?"

He smiled. "Tribesmen are experts with fire."

She rolled her eyes at him then started gutting the fish.

Still dripping water and mud, Elice walked over to them. Without warning, the water exploded from her skin in a puff of dirty snow, which she shook all over Sakari and Adar.

"Hey!" Sakari protested. Plopping down beside her, Elice grinned. Sakari scooped up a handful of mud and smeared it on Elice's cheek. "There. That will protect you from any surviving mosquitoes." In response, Elice threw a clot of mud at Sakari, and then the three of them were throwing mud and laughing till their sides ached.

They finished cleaning the fish and roasted them over the smoky fire. It was a simple meal, but Adar had never tasted anything so good. "I swear, I'll never eat raw meat or drink blood again."

On the mossy ground, the three friends lay side by side, Adar and Sakari holding Elice's hands to keep the cold at bay. Though the clouds had fled, the chill still lingered. Adar wondered if he'd ever escape it entirely as he stared up at the midnight sun. It was never fully dark this far north, with the sun circling in an off-kilter loop above them. From the other side of Elice, Sakari started snoring softly.

"Do you think Aklaq and his dogs are all right?" Elice asked quietly so as not to wake her friend.

Adar hoped so—the man had risked his life to help them escape. "He knows how to survive the queendom—better even than we do."

"Do you think my mother will hurt him for helping me?" Her voice was barely over a whisper.

The truth was, Adar didn't know. But what was another lie at this point? "No. I don't think Ilyenna will hurt him."

She didn't relax at his words. "My magic is weaker here— almost sluggish. It frightens me to feel so powerless."

"I felt the same way in the queendom," Adar replied, then realized he might have said too much. He tried to stave off the urge to warn her. Tried and failed. "I'm afraid your magic will continue to grow weaker."

She shifted to face him. "How do you know?"

"Because the farther you travel from the source of winter's power, the harder it will be to draw from it."

He felt her studying him and wondered if she could see the sweat on his brow. "How do you know so much?" she asked.

"Same way you knew what a tree looks like even though you've never seen one. Books." Against all odds, Adar had escaped the Winter Queendom with Elice. He was near the fire again, and his belly was full. But he didn't let himself feel the happiness, the relief. He knew it couldn't last. Instead, dread welled up where the joy could have been. Fire and burning, how could he make her see?

"After my ship sank, I thought I would never leave the queendom alive. I didn't think this far ahead . . . I didn't consider the consequences. Not like I should have."

Her hand felt for his, her palm cool against his warmth. "What happens now?" she asked.

"You come with me to my home." There had never been any question about that.

Elice scratched at the mosquito bites on her cheek. "Are you asking me to go with you to the Adrack? That's dangerously close to Idara."

Adar faced her, letting her see the earnestness in his gaze. "I'll look after you. I swear I will."

She bit her lip, drawing his attention to the full bottom lip that drove him crazy. "I never thought to trade one desert for another. I always wanted to go somewhere green. Somewhere like the clanlands. I have family there."

He glanced away to hide the guilt in his eyes. "We don't have to decide right now. First, we need to get Sakari safely to her family. We owe her at least that much. After that . . ." Adar couldn't finish his thought.

Elice sighed and snuggled up to him, resting her head on his chest. He wrapped an arm around her, and she fell asleep almost instantly. He knew she trusted him. Completely. The wind shifted her hair so it tickled his face, but he did not move it away. Instead, he held her tighter.

For five days, Sakari, Adar, and Elice traveled across the marshy tundra. For five days Adar watched Elice. She radiated joy, the grin hardly ever slipping from her face. She exclaimed over animals she'd rarely, if ever, seen in the Winter Queendom foxes and eagles, caribou and muskoxen, rabbits and ermine, bobcats and lemmings. When the group stopped to rest, Elice chattered on while Adar wrapped her bloody feet in strips of fabric. Sakari worked at turning a brace of rabbits she'd caught into a pair of boots to replace the ones Elice had lost to the river.

Despite the incessant mosquitoes and the cuts on her feet, Elice cheerfully rubbed Adar's nearly healed shoulder—an injury left over from the sinking ship she'd rescued him from—and rested her cool hands on the knot on Sakari's head. Elice kept asking them questions about the world around them until Adar really, really wanted to put those lips to another use. But he didn't. He patiently answered every question, though he didn't have nearly as many answers as Sakari.

On the fifth day they reached the coast, where the gray ocean spread before them, its matte surface unmarred by a single piece of ice. As they traveled along the windy shore, Adar kept his head tucked in his hood, wondering how he was ever going to make any of this right.

He was so deep in thought he didn't notice Elice until she was tugging at his sleeve. "I said, what is that?"

He looked around, realizing Sakari had gone off somewhere. The hilly land surrounded a picturesque little bay. Adar followed Elice's gesture to see something dark and heavily textured on one side. "Trees."

She squealed in delight and took off running. Adar watched her, black hair streaming behind her as she raced up the coast. When she realized he wasn't following, she spun back, her hair flaring around her radiant face. "Adar, I'm going to see real trees!"

He couldn't help but smile, his insides nearly bursting to see her so happy. He wanted nothing more than to make her that happy for the rest of his life. But then his grin slipped off, because he couldn't deny it anymore. He loved her. So much it hurt.

Elice sprinted ahead, barely daring to blink as she watched the dark texture take on a green tint. Appearing between the trunks were clumps of white, which she gradually recognized as patches of snow, preserved by the shade of the trees. She imagined she could smell them—the sharp sweet smell her grandfather had told her about.

Then she could make out their branches, coated with dark-green needles that looked like rime frost, formed when wind drove freezing fog and left behind needlelike projections, almost like thousands of little spears. When Elice stood before them, she gazed up at their impressive height, awestruck.

She stepped forward as if in a trance, took hold of a branch, and pulled off some of the needles. She inhaled the fragrance. It was sharp and deep, just like her grandfather had said. She wished he was with her now—he must miss the outside world so terribly. She tucked the needles into the front of her robes and held her fingers by her nose, inhaling the scent lingering on her fingers.

"We can camp here for tonight," Adar said.

Elice turned to see Adar behind her, watching her sadly. Wanting him to feel some of the joy bursting through her, she took hold of his hand and they wandered through the conifer forest with its springy floor of pine needles. She could still taste winter here. And if she closed her eyes, she could almost pretend she was back in her own forest, her grandfather just out of sight.

They built another fire in an empty space between the trees and the ocean. Sakari had found some fresh leaves with a strange, crunchy texture, and a stillborn, freshly-dead caribou calf that they roasted over the fire.

Elice tried many times to get Adar to talk to her, but he kept giving her single-syllable answers before staring off into the dark forest again. Sakari was quiet, too. Elice wanted nothing more than to share the magic of sleeping before a real forest, but her friends seemed too preoccupied.

Giving up on Adar, she sat beside Sakari and asked, "What's the matter?"

Sakari's brows furrowed. "I hurried ahead this morning because I thought I recognized this place. I thought there was a village nearby that I used to visit as a child. But instead I found this bay. So now I'm not sure where we are."

Elice looked around, noting the way the light reflected off the gentle waves. "We're bound to get there soon."

Sakari swallowed. "That's part of what makes me so scared. I've been gone nearly five years. A lot can change in that much time. What if my grandparents are dead? What if they don't want me? What if I came all this way only to find I was running toward nothing?"

"Love isn't something that fades with time. It just grows sharper with longing." Elice looped her arm through Sakari's. "And if they are gone, you can come with me to the clanlands."

Sakari's gaze shifted to Adar. "I would be in the way." Elice shot her an annoyed glance. Sakari threw up her hands. "I've seen the way you two look at each other."

Elice sighed. "He's been . . . different since we passed into summer. Each day it feels like he's withdrawing a little more."

Sakari took a deep breath. "It will sort itself out."

"And if I don't want to go with him to the desert?"

"You don't have to decide today." Sakari rose to her feet and held out a hand. "I'm going to bed. You coming?"

Elice stared out over the water. "Not yet. I want to go for a swim first."

After Sakari slipped out of sight, Elice stripped down to her underdress. She moved to where the water lapped against her toes, the frigid kiss like coming home. After encasing her head in an ice bubble, she picked up a rock and slipped into the briny water.

What she saw surprised her. There were trees under the water—she hadn't known they grew there. She formed flippers and kicked through the trees, which looked just like the conifer forest she'd seen before. She reached out to break off some needles, but instead of snapping off in her hand, they were soft and flexible—almost spongy.

Elice kept swimming, shocked to see flowering plants and grass and lichen just like on shore. She didn't know the seabed outside of her palace, but something about this felt wrong, unnatural.

She swam on and was studying the swaying grass before her when she bumped into something. She hauled herself back and looked up. And screamed. She dropped her rock and hauled herself back, arms and legs franticly pumping. Before her was a young girl of maybe seven. Her eyes were open and sightless, her thick hair shifting with the currents. Her skin was just beginning to slough off. Beyond the girl was a whole village, houses still standing. There were caribou and dogs and hundreds of people—all of them dead.

Heart pounding, Elice kicked hard for the distant surface. The moment she reached it, her ice bubble shattered and she started screaming, kicking for the shore as she went.

Adar and Sakari sprang up and ran halfway out into the water. "Elice!" Adar cried.

She was sobbing so hard she could barely swim. He dove in after her while Sakari paced and wrung her hands. Elice tried to swim toward Adar, but she kept imagining the dead below her. Imagining them reaching for her with their too-pale hands, the skin falling off.

She went under, choking on her sobs, clawing at the ocean that refused to let her go. And then Adar's arms were around her. He pulled her up above the water, his arm pinned around her chest. "Hang on."

She sank against his warm skin as he kicked for shore. When it was deep enough to stand, Sakari met them to help take Elice to the fire. Sakari scoured her dry with her caribou coat and then flipped it inside out and rested it against her. Then she started rubbing Elice's arms. Elice didn't need the warmth, but she was desperate for the comfort.

Adar threw more wood on the fire, and suddenly it surged hot and bright. He turned to Elice and asked, "What happened?"

Shivering, she looked into Sakari's eyes. "You were right. This is where the village was. It's still there. Just beneath the surface."

Elice was subdued the next day. Though she didn't need the warmth, she had Sakari's coat wrapped tightly around her for the comfort it offered. Adar stayed at Elice's side, his expression closed off. Elice didn't understand his standoffishness. And she was too shaken to try to draw him out. Sakari scouted ahead, desperate for signs of the village she remembered from childhood. Unspoken between the three friends was the fear that Sakari's village had been destroyed, just like the last one.

The landscape had grown steadily hillier, almost mountainous, and the forests were thick now. Elice, Adar, and Sakari climbed one last hill and finally glimpsed a village beside a river. They started their descent and soon could see the details of the village's log houses. When they were close enough to start making out faces, Sakari froze, her chest heaving. She whirled around to meet Elice's gaze. "That house—the closest one to us and the river—is my grandparents' house!" Sakari turned back, trembling with excitement. "And that's them!"

She took off, calling her grandparents' names. Two gray-haired people glanced up from their garden, shading their eyes against the glare. The woman dropped her basket and rushed forward, the man close behind. They wrapped Sakari in their arms and murmured happily to her in Svass.

When Sakari's grandparents asked about her father, mother, and younger brothers, she started crying. Her grandparents joined in the mourning. Elice felt like an intruder here. She started backing away and soon she and Adar wandered to the river and sat on the bank, the rushing sound of the water soothing her senses.

After a few minutes, Adar spoke. "If you could have saved Sakari's family, or that village we saw yesterday, would you?"

"Of course," Elice replied.

He stared at his clasped hands. "What if you had to risk your own life to do it?"

"Isn't that what I did when I saved Aklaq's village?" Elice wondered what he was getting at.

Adar finally met her gaze. "What if you could save a hundred thousand villages? What if to do that, all you had to do was sacrifice someone you loved?"

She shook her head. "I don't understand."

"What if the Sundering is real, Elice? What would you give up to save all these people from dying?"

Her mouth fell open, but she couldn't think of the words to fill it. She shook her head and tried again. "*If* it was real, I don't know."

His head fell forward, as if it were too heavy to hold up.

She rested a hand on his back. "Adar? What is it?"

Elice turned at the sound of someone coming through the brush. Sakari appeared, giving them a watery smile. "I want you to meet my grandparents."

Feeling hesitant, Elice turned back to Adar. He gave her a halfhearted smile. "Come on. We traveled all this way to see Sakari safely with her family. Can't miss it now."

Back at the little log cabin, Elice and Adar were introduced to Sakari's grandparents, Yalgar and Mab. The inside of their cabin was dark and smoky and smelled like fish. Mab fed them fish stew flavored with spring onions. From her place beside Sakari, Elice said, "You're staying." It was not a question. She could see the relief in the other girl's expression.

Sakari rested her forehead on Elice's shoulder. "I'm not choking on ashes anymore. A lot of that has to do with your friendship. I don't want you to leave me, but this is my home—as the forever ice never was."

Elice laid her head on top of Sakari's. "I think the Shyle might be that for me—though I have never been there."

"Places keep pieces of us, like roots planted in soil. We can take a seed somewhere else, but our roots remain."

"Trees don't grow in the queendom." Elice knew the forest she had created was nothing but an illusion, a poor mimic of reality. But her grandfather had planted her roots deep in the Shyle in a way she would never be rooted in the queendom.

"I know," Sakari said.

Elice looked up. "Where did Adar go?"

Sakari followed her gaze. "He must've slipped out. Something's . . . off about him lately."

Elice could only nod in agreement.

The next few hours passed in a blur of Sakari's extended family members. They all brought Sakari gifts—useful things like hide clothing, a serviceable knife, and even a black pot. It was dark but warm inside the cabin, and Elice felt more at ease knowing the fairies wouldn't bother her in her sleep because of the smoke. She realized she hadn't seen a single summer fairy yet, which seemed odd, since summer supported much more life than winter did. Then again she'd never been inside summer before. Maybe fairies were different here. Maybe her Sight only worked with winter fairies. She determined to ask Adar tomorrow and promptly fell asleep.

When Elice woke the next morning, he was tugging his shirt over his bare chest. He grabbed a slice of bread from the table and headed for the door. She propped herself up on one elbow. "Where are you headed this early?" she whispered so as not to wake the others.

Adar started and glanced back at her. "I've been seeing about passage out of Svass."

She yawned. "We haven't discussed whether we're leaving yet. I'd like to stay with Sakari for a while."

"Spend the day with her. Have fun. I'll see you again tonight."

Elice started to protest, but Adar opened the door and slipped away before she got the words out. She cast an annoyed look at the closed door, then pushed her way out of the blankets and took a slice of bread and dried fish for her breakfast. As she ate, she glanced around the single room, at the old couple near the fire. At Sakari's serene face.

Wanting to thank these people for their kindness and give Sakari something to remember her by, Elice set aside her half-finished meal. Her fingers remembered how to fold and bend the ice, how to shape it. On her first try, she had a tree nearly the length of her arm with strong roots. She tied the ice's connection to winter, so it would never melt. Then she studied her creation. It was beautiful and proportional, with the intricate roots from which the tree stood as the focal point.

Satisfied, Elice picked up her bread and fish and leaned back. But before she could take another bite, something caught the corner of her eye. She turned to find the old couple and Sakari sitting up in their furs, watching her.

Mab pressed a hand to her chest. "Who have you brought us, Sakari?"

Sakari answered, "Elice is the daughter of winter."

Elice tensed, waiting for the same anger she'd seen from Aklaq's village. But Yalgar only inclined his head. "You are most welcome, daughter of winter."

She gave a small smile. "I made this for you," she said to Sakari. "It will never melt."

"The roots," Sakari replied, her eyes shining. She pushed back her furs and hurried over to embrace Elice.

"Well, the least I can do after such a gift is make you a fine breakfast," Mab declared.

They ate fried fish and cooked greens for breakfast. Elice told Sakari's family what the Winter Palace looked like. Then Sakari and Elice stepped into the early morning sunshine.

Elice couldn't help but look around for Adar, but he was nowhere to be seen. Sakari took Elice's hand and they hurried to the other side of the village. Beyond the forest was an open tundra. A dozen boys mounted on caribou tended the villagers' herd.

Elice gaped at them. "I didn't know people rode caribou!"

Sakari grinned. "Want to try?"

Elice bit the inside of her cheek. "Yes."

The boys eagerly agreed, showing Elice how to steer with the reins attached to a hackamore, which they explained was like a bridle but without the metal piece that went in the animal's mouth. But she hesitated before climbing into the vibrant cloth-covered saddle. "What if I get impaled by the antlers?"

Sakari laughed. "You wanted to experience summer, remember?"

Not entirely convinced, Elice put her left foot in the stirrup and mounted the beast. As one of the boys led the caribou around, Elice's body rocked back and forth with the animal's gait. Grateful the caribou hadn't reared back to stab her with an antler, she reached down and patted its fur, which felt rough and spindly with a downy layer beneath. She was surprised by the clicking sound the reindeer's legs made with each step.

Just when Elice was starting to relax a little, the boy handed her the reins and smacked the caribou's backside, sending it running across the tundra. Elice clung to the reins as she was violently tossed from side to side on the saddle. Then she gave up and bailed off. She hit the ground hard.

She waited for a moment to see if anything hurt, but the spongy ground had softened her fall. She looked up in time to see Sakari smack the grin off the boy's face. Then Sakari came to help Elice to her feet. "Are you all right?"

Elice brushed herself off, then held out a palm and filled it with swirls of snow. "Should I freeze him?"

The boy gaped at her, turned on his heel, and ran. Elice waited as long as she could before bursting into laughter. Sakari joined in and managed to say, "He won't try that again."

Elice looked after the retreating caribou. "How will he ever catch it?"

"That's his problem." Sakari chuckled.

Back at the village, strings of rope were being set out with wood beneath them to smoke fish. Apparently, the salmon run would start any day. The fish would surge into the bay and up the rivers. People would catch them by the hundreds and dry them over the fires, or pack them in sealskins sealed up with fat. According to Sakari, the fermented results of packing the fish were delicious.

Thinking of the delicious fish stew she'd had yesterday, Elice planned to eat until her belly burst. More than one woman had commented that it was time to put on her summer fat. Elice wandered along the bay, watching for the fish. Across the wide river, she noticed large brown bears waiting as well. When she expressed concern to Mab, the old woman smiled and said, "They have their side of the river and we have ours. But if you do happen upon one, just back away slowly. They're here for the fish, not us."

Everyone in the cabin was awakened very early the next morning by shouts of excitement. Adar was there—Elice had only seen him in passing yesterday. She briefly wondered if he was ignoring her, but the three Svass were already hurrying out of the house.

She hustled after them and moved to Adar's side. "Are you avoiding me?"

He shot her a confused look. "What? No, I just thought you'd want to spend as much time with Sakari as possible before we leave."

Elice frowned. "I haven't said I'm coming with you. And it's not like you aren't her friend too."

He pointed. "Look at that."

Frustrated that he'd changed the subject, Elice followed his gaze to see the river teeming with fish.

"Come on!" Adar jogged ahead, joining the rush of people heading to the river.

She stared after him before throwing her hands in the air and hurrying after him. She worked with Mab, Yalgar, Sakari, and Adar, spreading wide nets that were almost instantly filled. The writhing fish were hauled back and dumped on the shore, where villagers went about clubbing the fishes' heads. They placed the catch on long tables, where the women filleted and boned the fish, then laid them out on drying racks. Everyone worked all day, until the salmon racks were filled.

That night, the men built huge bonfires and smaller cooking fires. The women brought out their kettles and filled them with fish, oysters, herbs, fresh vegetables, and broth. Bubbling happily over the fires, the stew permeated the air with a mouthwatering aroma.

While they waited, Sakari braided Elice's hair and added an iridescent black feather with a strand of beads that tinkled beside her ear. Sakari even convinced her grandmother to lend Elice a white deerskin dress and matching boots. Elice felt beautiful and alive, like the fire crackling in front of them. She had never felt so happy, so accepted, as she did in that moment. The urge to thank this village swelled within her. She moved away from the firelight, to a small rise hidden from sight by the forest. And there she created her own tree, a replica of the one she'd made for Sakari.

When Elice returned to the dancing, the old woman brought bowls of soup to her and Sakari. Elice blew the steam from it until it was cool enough to eat. The myriad of flavors were completely unexpected, the heat blending them and sharpening them in ways she wouldn't have imagined.

Men brought out drums and beat a steady rhythm. Some of the village girls started to dance. Elice had just lined up for her third bowl of soup when Sakari grabbed her arm and hauled her toward the dancers. Elice hesitated before joining in. The beads tinkled in her ear, the feather brushing against her face. The food warmed her belly, and her feet seemed to move in rhythm to her heart. She looked around and caught Adar's gaze. She motioned for him to join her, but he shook his head. Elice danced over to him and tried again. Instead, he took her hand and led her away from the firelight.

"Where are we going?" she asked, breathless from exertion.

"I wanted to show you something."

She followed him into the soften dusk of a northern summer night, dark enough to dim the colors but still light enough to see clearly. He paused. Elice glanced around but saw only trees and bushes and ferns. She turned back to him expectantly.

Adar pulled something out of his pocket and held it out to her. "I wanted to say thank you." She stared at the leather cord with a turquoise spiral at the center. "I traded my caribou clothes for it. We won't need them anymore."

From the twilight sky, Elice could make out the gold strands throughout the stone, running through it like lightning across the sunlight sky.

"If you don't like it, I could probably get you something else," Adar finally said.

She started out of her examination. "I was beginning to think you were angry with me."

"Never." He gave her a shy smile. "The colors—it reminded me of you." He held out the stone and she took it, noticing it still held the warmth from his body. It nestled on her chest beside the flower her grandfather had given her.

"I know it's not the jewels you are used to, but . . ."

He didn't get a chance to finish, because Elice leaned forward and pressed her lips to his. She pulled back almost as quickly, startled that she'd kissed him. "I'm sorry, I didn't mean—"

Adar stared at her, his face conflicted. "Elly . . ."

She bit the inside of her cheek. "What is it?"

He kicked angrily at the ground. "I'm not worthy of you."

She laughed. "Because you're not a prince?" He winced. "Well, I'm not a princess, not anymore. For the first time in my life, I'm just Elice."

He pressed his forehead to hers and cupped her cheek, his thumb stroking little lines of fire that spread just under her skin. He made no move to kiss her again, though she could tell he wanted to. Why was he being so reluctant?

Wetting her lips, she took a tiny step forward so her body was flush against Adar's. She could feel the hardness of his chest, the strength that seemed to pulse from deep inside him. She reached out to run her fingers along his scruffy jawline and then up toward his hair.

He caught her hand and held it against him. "Elly, you'll regret this tomorrow."

She pressed kisses to the places her fingers had touched, the stubble rough under her sensitive lips. "No. I won't. But you might if you don't kiss me back."

With a groan, Adar slid his fingers through her hair. Then he cupped the back of her head and pulled her face to his. His mouth moved over hers slowly, gently. It was the first time Elice had ever kissed a man, but she learned quickly. And when the kiss deepened, she was ready, her mouth opening to his tongue. She'd never felt so warm, the heat building up inside of her like a delicious burn.

Then he halted abruptly and tucked her head under his chin. "Elly." His voice was rough and low, and she could feel him straining to control himself.

"I don't want to stop," she said breathlessly.

"No. Just no." Adar kissed her forehead before stepping back. The cool air shivered between them.

Elice wrapped her arms around herself. "Why are you rejecting me?"

"I love you, Elly," he said softly. "Fire and burning, I do. That's why I'm not going to take advantage of you now. I'm not going to let you do something I know you'll regret later."

Her mouth parted in disbelief. "You love me?"

He slowly nodded. "If you still want me tomorrow, I'm all yours." He held out his hand to her. She took it, as she had done a hundred times before. His hand fit perfectly inside her own.

"I can't imagine a world where I don't want you every single day, Adar."

He winced—not the reaction she'd expected. He led her back to the circle of firelight. Sakari shot them a knowing glance that made Elice blush and cover her mouth with her hand, wondering if people could tell by the tender look of her lips that Adar had just kissed her senseless.

Elice stared up at him, but his gaze was fixed on something on the other side of the fire, his expression dark. "What's wrong?" she asked as she followed his line of sight.

He stepped in front of her, blocking her view. "Nothing. Why don't you go dance with Sakari again. I want to get more soup."

She noted the stiff set of his shoulders, but his expression pled for her to trust him. And she did. "I'll see you soon?" But he was already turning away and didn't seem to hear her question.

All around Elice were dozens of smiling faces. Some of the village girls took hold of her hands and spun round and round the bonfire, giggling and laughing. The feather and beads in Elice's hair twirled, dozens of dazzling colors she could just make out from the corners of her eyes.

The music wove around them, intoxicating, filling the hollow spaces where only silence had been. Elice drew it into her—the songs, the energy of the crowd, the laughter of the other girls, the way the dark trees framed the star-strewn sky. And she realized she need never go back—never live through another winter of darkness. Never ache with the sound of silence.

She longed to touch Adar, to share with him the dance she'd learned. She managed to slip away from the other girls to search for him. Curving through the crowd, she sought out his familiar face. She caught sight of his dark head disappearing into the forest and sped after him. She crossed into the trees and stepped over a mossy log. The ground was spongy and damp, and wet leaves brushed across her face. "Adar?" she called.

No response, but Elice caught a flash of his pale shirt. She lifted her dress and rushed after him, leaving behind the blaring music and the light of the fire. The farther she walked, the deeper and darker the forest became. Water from the trees dripped onto her, great plunking drops that shivered down her scalp and seeped through her clothing.

She reached the edge of the clearing, the perpetual twilight lighting up what lay before her. Adar stood in the clearing, his back to her. A bright smile stole over Elice's face and then faded. He was whispering to . . . nothing? She stepped closer. And then she saw it. A fairy with spider wings, and a stack of eyes atop her head.

"I don't answer to you," Adar said belligerently. The fairy murmured, too softly for Elice to hear. "Just give me a little more time," Adar snapped.

Elice took another step forward and could finally make out the fairy's words. "Time for what, princeling? The girl is already ours." The spider fairy's voice sounded oddly sticky. When Adar didn't answer, the fairy sneered, "If you refuse to answer to me, you will answer to her."

"Do you really want to test me, Tix?" Adar said. A bright flame hovered over his hand. Elice was unable to stop a gasp from leaving her lips. Adar jerked around, harsh shadows cast over his face by the firelight.

Suddenly, that sticky voice was coming from over Elice's shoulder. "Oh, she smells like winter." Elice craned her head back and saw a spindly spider the size of her palm on her shoulder blade. She shrieked and tried to brush it off. But the spider laughed and skittered up her head, clinging onto her hair.

"Yesssss, ice and snow and the sea. You did indeed find her, princeling."

A blast of flame shot from Adar's hand, knocking the spider off Elice's head. In an instant, the spider fairy lit up.

She laughed, her legs cavorting in her death throes. "You'll pay for that," she said just before she died.

Gasping in a breath that tasted of burnt hair, Elice gaped at Adar. All the times he'd asked after the princess, all the times he'd tried to convince Elice to leave the queendom. The way he always kept his hair pulled tightly back or covered by a ridiculous hat, as if to hide the tattoos the Idarans wore on their scalps. She thought of how sullen and withdrawn he'd become of late. "You're not a tribesman. You're an Idaran."

Adar pressed his mouth shut and used his hand to snuff out the flame. "Elly, please, let me explain."

"You're the Summer Queen's son. No one else could have power over fire."

He held out his hand imploringly. "I promise this isn't what it looks like."

Winter raged into Elice, snow sparking from her fingertips. "You lured me away from the safety of the queendom!" He winced, but didn't deny it. Frost spread around the ferns at Elice's feet, looking like delicate lace. As she stepped back, the leaves shattered with a tinkling sound. "Why?" Her voice shook under the weight of despair. All the stories, all the warnings her mother had ever given her pounded in her head. "Do you think to use me to get back at my mother?"

Adar glanced at the frost spreading around him and climbing up the trees until the whole clearing was encased in hoarfrost. "Fire and burning, Elice, I didn't want you to find out like this."

"You lied to me. All along, you've lied to me." Furious tears streamed down her cheeks.

"I tried to talk you out of coming with me," he finally admitted, his gaze locked on hers. "But now"—he shrugged helplessly—"it's too late."

A little more sluggishly than usual, an ice spear formed in one of Elice's hands, a dart in the other. "Too late for what?"

"Elly, no one is going to hurt you."

He reached toward her with the same hand that had held the flames. She dropped into a fighter's stance—the stance her father had taught her.

Adar froze. "Don't."

She lunged, flinging her ice dart at him. A wave of something hit her dart, melting it so it only splashed his clothing. He hadn't even moved. "Elice, please, we don't have to do this!"

She launched her ice spear at him. "Melt that!"

He threw a ball of fire that collided with her spear. Hissing steam pushed toward him, while glittering frost shifted back to her. "All I've ever wanted to do is end the war between our families," Adar declared. "Bringing you here will accomplish that."

Elice formed another spear and launched herself at him. He threw a ball of fire. It slammed into her shield and melted it down to the handle. She threw it at him, satisfied when it grazed his cheek, drawing a line of blood. She drove her spear at him, but it hit a shield of heat and melted to a stub. This too she tossed at Adar. She feinted a jab at his right side before swinging her fist against his injured shoulder. He twisted, taking the blow to his back, and dropped. He aimed a sweeping kick at her ankles. Elice jumped, kicking at his head. His hand snaked out, grabbed her foot, and jerked her forward.

She landed hard and tried to scramble to her feet. But Adar was quick. He landed on top of her, pinning her two hands with just one of his. "You said you practically grew up in a library!" she shrieked at him.

He winced again. "I also said I was a warrior. The priestesses trained me in combat."

The cold raged from Elice's skin. Adar's mouth tightened, and she felt heat waves radiating from him to negate her cold.

"Fire and burning, Elly, just listen to me!"

She squirmed, hating the feel of his body on top of hers, his heat pressing down on her. "You've done nothing but lie to me! Why would I believe anything you say now?"

He let out a long, exasperated breath. "Think! I could have killed you a hundred times. I could have called for my mother the moment we left the Winter Queendom. But I didn't."

Elice struggled against him, but his grip felt like iron. "I don't believe you."

"Doesn't matter." He clenched his jaw. "It's better if she doesn't know I care about you. She won't trust me if she thinks my reasoning is compromised. But I promise, no one is going to hurt you."

"And my mother?" Elice choked.

Adar's expression hardened. "If she cooperates, nothing will happen to her, either."

Before Elice could respond, she became aware of a rushing sound, rhythmic and loud. She knew that sound, because it had filled her with both longing and dread her entire life. The sound of enormous wings. She struggled hard, fear choking her. Because now that sound meant death. For her entire life she'd known the Summer Queen would kill her if she ever got the chance. "Adar, please . . ."

"Pretend you hate me." His expression went unreadable as he looked up to greet his mother. But suddenly a shadow moved behind him, and he collapsed on top of Elice with a moan.

A hand hauled him back, revealing Sakari's shadowed face. She held a large branch in her fist. "Run!" she commanded.

Elice sprang to her feet. Giving into blind fear, she crashed through the meadow and stumbled through the shadows, Sakari right beside her. They had almost reached the trees when vines shot out and snatched their legs. Both young women hit the ground hard. Momentarily stunned, Elice glanced up to see a fairy grinning as more vines tightened around Elice and Sakari. The sound of wings had grown louder now, nearly right on top of them.

Drawing deep from winter, Elice sent out a blast of cold that froze the whole clearing in an instant. The fairy's face contorted in a rictus of horror. The vines holding Elice turned brittle and broke as she struggled to free herself. She hauled Sakari to her feet and braced herself to run, but a wall of flames erupted before them. Elice staggered back, squinting at the writhing fire. All around her, the frost melted, leaving everything limp and dead.

Adar had done this. He had stopped her. "It's too late," she heard him say.

Fairies converged on Elice. More vines shot out, wrapping her so tight they actually lifted her off the ground, her arms and legs spread out. A moment later, a flash of orange-and-gold fire shot across the horizon, growing bigger and brighter by the moment.

Elice watched in horror as the Summer Queen flared her fiery wings and dropped to the ground in a crouch. She looked up, her expression as blank as her son's. Like Adar, Nelay had dark features and a cunning glint to her eyes.

"Mother," he said. "Meet Elice, daughter of winter."

The Summer Queen rose to her feet, her gaze never leaving Elice. "She has her mother's eyes." She nodded to the fairies controlling the vines. "You have done well. You shall be rewarded."

Calling the full fury of winter to her, Elice struggled to break free. But a simple gesture from Nelay reduced winter to a trickle. "Winter has no place here. Not now." She drew a curving sword from a cross baldric on her back, then stalked forward. The sword's sapphires and rubies glinted along the flat side of the blade.

Elice felt a sob building in her throat. She was going to die. But the queen paused before Sakari. "Who is this?"

Adar stepped up beside Sakari. "She helped us escape the queendom. I wouldn't have survived without her."

Nelay lifted her curving sword and brought it down in a rush of silver. Elice screamed. But Nelay had only cut the vine holding Sakari's wrist. With quick chops, the Summer Queen freed the girl's other hand and her feet.

"Be gone," Nelay told Sakari. "And when Ilyenna comes, tell her we have her daughter. I will meet with her in the usual place to discuss her surrender."

Sakari shot a questioning look at Elice, who knew she would fight if Elice asked her to. "Go." Elice choked on a sob, not sure what to say to the friend she would probably never see again.

Sakari turned furious eyes to Adar and spit on him. The moisture bubbled and hissed on his skin, but he made no move to retaliate. Sakari turned on her heel and hurried away.

"Make sure she doesn't return," Nelay said, and Tix clicked her fangs at something out of sight.

Nelay shifted her unfeeling gaze back to Elice. "If you stake out a lamb on a hill, the wolves will come." The Summer Queen spoke to another fairy that hovered at her shoulder, its black scales shining in the moonlight. "Render her harmless."

The fairy shot forward and sank its fangs into Elice's shoulder. She recoiled at the bite's sting, then gasped at the fire burning through her veins.

Nelay cut her free, and Elice staggered as her legs again took her weight. Her blood felt thick and sluggish. Her knees buckled and she sank to the ground. With the last of her strength, she ripped the necklace from her throat and threw it at Adar, feeling a moment of satisfaction when he flinched. Then Elice's head was too heavy to hold up. She collapsed back, barely managing to keep her glare fixed on Adar.

His mother clapped a hand on his arm. "This is why you always win the game of fire. This is why you will win the War of the Queens for me."

"You vastly overestimate my mother's affection." Elice scoffed. She wondered if her mother would feel anything at all when she learned of her daughter's capture.

Nelay crouched beside Elice and studied her face. "You have your father's curls and the shape of his eyes," she said finally. "Your mother will come." Nelay rose and pivoted, gesturing to the fairies. "Take her to Thanjavar." The queen's wings of fire unfurled from her back. "Quickly. Her mother's spies might already know we have her."

"How many must die before you stop this?" Elice said as she struggled to keep her eyes open.

Nelay looked down at her. "I didn't start this war. But I will finish it." Then hundreds of fairies converged on Elice, blocking out everything else.

Long after midnight, the net carried by a thousand fairies settled Adar on top of the observation tower in the palatial compound of Thanjavar. He scrambled to free himself. Ignoring the cramps in his calves, he headed straight to his apartments on the second floor of the palace. He changed into his fighting clothes—loose, dark robes that tied together with a pleated fabric belt. His shoulder ached as he laced his boots and armed himself with his double-cross baldric and a half dozen knives. Feeling more in control than he had in weeks, he stormed from his rooms, glaring at anyone who dared approach him.

He stalked through the darkness, heading straight for his family's quarters down another corridor. The Summer Queen's guards wore a special sun emblem, meaning they were under her control and not that of Idara's queen, Parisa, who lived on the coast in the capitol city of Mubia.

"I need to speak with the goddess," Adar told his mother's guards.

They bowed from the shoulders. "She has gone to Commander Jezzel's quarters, my prince."

Adar pivoted without another word. He was halfway to Jezzel's apartments when he saw the faint blue light of one of his mother's fires. He slowed his steps and peered down the corridor to find his mother and Jezzel, heads bent together in furtive whispers, the blue nimbus above them casting harsh shadows across their faces. Anyone seeing them for the first time would merely see two girls no more than eighteen years old, whispering palace gossip or lamenting an assignment from one of their teachers. No one would ever guess both women were over forty years old. Or that Nelay had eighteen children. Or that the enormously pregnant Jezzel was days away from being a grandmother.

As the Fairy Queen, his mother had granted immortality to Jezzel and to Adar's father, Rycus. Every year, each received a single petal from an elice blossom. Only one bloomed per year, producing just three petals. The third was saved for emergencies; Adar had received one himself, after his chariot accident. And the time before that, when he'd been shot in the back by a crossbolt. Since then, he'd never had so much as a sniffle, and he healed remarkably fast.

Now he stepped closer to hear the conversation between his mother and Jezzel.

"You will do as I say," Nelay said, her tone hard. She held out a single elice petal, white with a burgundy center.

Jezzel crossed her arms over her chest. "I have been your commander for twenty years. I'm tired of war and death and blood. Cinab is now twice my age, and my daughter is older than I am. She will give birth any day. Someday that child will be older than me, as well. And sometime after that, they will all be dead. I don't want to be young anymore, not if it means being left behind by my family."

"Adar is older than I am," Nelay admitted. "But you don't see me giving up."

Jezzel huffed. "Can you bear to watch him grow old and die while you remain forever young?"

Nelay glanced away. "I don't have a choice."

"But I do. And I've made my choice. It's over, Nelay. We made our gambit and we lost. I won't take my petal. I'm going to have this baby in whatever peace I can find."

Adar had never seen Jezzel so despondent, or his mother so desperate.

"You would leave me alone?"

"You've never been alone, Nelay. You have Rycus, and he will never leave you."

Nelay stared at her friend, pleading in her gaze. Seeming to soften a bit, Jezzel murmured, "I'll still be here. I just won't be commanding the armies anymore."

Nelay leaned forward to rest one of her hands over her friend's. "Just trust me once more. After this it will be over, I promise."

Jezzel eyed her. "You have another plan, don't you?"

"I always do. Come with me."

They turned up the corridor, heading straight for Adar. Before he could duck back out of sight, his mother spotted him and threw a nimbus of light in his direction. He shielded himself from the brightness.

"Adar?" The ball traveled back up the ceiling. Nelay relaxed her grip on her sword and tucked the petal back into her robes.

He squared his shoulders, then stepped into the light and gave his mother a small bow. "I've just arrived. Where is Elice being kept?"

"Somewhere safe." His mother's eyes narrowed as she studied him.

"I hear you actually went to the Winter Palace," Jezzel said with a hint of amusement. "What was it like?"

"Cold," Adar replied.

Jezzel rolled her eyes. "You know what I meant."

"There isn't much evidence of the Sundering in the queendom. Not so for Svass. Many people have died." There.

He'd delivered his report. Now on to what he really wanted to know. "Where is Elice?"

"Safe and well cared for. Go get some rest. We plan to meet with the girl tomorrow after the midday meal. You'll see her then." Nelay's gaze locked on Adar's bare arm and pulled it into the light. She clucked over the new, rough scar from the seal bite.

He tried to quash the flutter of red fire that flared along his arm, but not before it had singed off the hair that had grown in over the last few months. His mother raised a single eyebrow as he pulled his arm back. Adar scowled in frustration. It had been years since he'd lost control like that. "I'd like to see her now," he said.

His mother shared a questioning look with Jezzel, then asked, "Why?"

Adar floundered for some explanation, some reason that didn't betray his feelings. But he couldn't find the words.

"Need I remind you what's at stake?" Nelay asked. She didn't need to, but that didn't stop her. "The Sundering is upon us. The destruction spreads by the day. You have brought me the tool I needed to end the destruction, but that's all Elice is—a tool."

"Ilyenna will have to agree to peace now." It was the reason Adar had gone to the queendom to fetch the Winter Queen's daughter.

"We've already treated with her, Son. She's banished Elice. Said we could keep her."

My fault, Adar thought bitterly. For a moment, all he could do was breathe. *So that's what they were talking about before. Why Jezzel was ready to give up.* "We'll find another way."

His mother folded her arms in front of her. "The players may be reset, but the game continues."

Adar clenched his fists behind his back so his mother and Jezzel wouldn't see. "How do you plan to use Elice now?"

Nelay made a sound low in her throat. "She's still our most powerful weapon. We just have to find another way to wield her."

Adar felt his fingernails cutting into his palms. "She's not a weapon—she's a woman. There has to be something we could give the Winter Queen to persuade her to make peace."

Nelay's head came up. "Do you think I will surrender? Abandon my realm to Ilyenna's fury as Leto did?" She moved closer, her words hot against Adar's face. "I will use Elice as I see fit."

His mother stepped past him without a backward glance. She and Jezzel headed down the corridor and turned toward the curving stairs, the guards following at a respectful distance.

Adar watched them go, his mind spinning with moves and countermoves. He had to know if Elice was safe—he was sick with worry over her. The only other way to do that would be to follow them. But he must be very careful. His mother always had spies, and if they suspected him, she'd know immediately.

To allay that suspicion, Adar created his own blue nimbus of light and held it out to illuminate the way as he trotted past his mother and Jezzel. He headed straight for the kitchens. Eating always threw fairies off, probably because the consumption of food was foreign to them. He grabbed the first edible thing he could find, a handful of figs, and popped them into his mouth one at a time. Then he grabbed a plate and filled it with some of the fruit, cheese, and bread left out by the cooks.

By the time Adar reached the main throne room, his mother and Jezzel were just heading out. He banished his nimbus and trailed behind them. Though he knew his mother's fairies watched him, he hoped they wouldn't find his behavior unusual enough to alert their queen to his presence.

Nelay and Jezzel moved into the courtyard. Adar tucked behind a phoenix statue and settled on the palace steps with his plate on his lap, pretending to look over the shadows of the city with its onion domes and empty markets. He ate his figs, a taste-less paste in his mouth, while watching his mother and Jezzel. They slipped into the library tower and disappeared from sight. Adar looked up at the five stories of smooth marble gleaming in the moonlight. There was no possibility of scaling the exterior, and no other path up besides the stairs.

Is Elice in the tower? Calculating the risks and rewards, he considered his options. He hadn't seen Elice since the night his mother had taken her. He'd spent three days in a net carried by fairies, trying to keep his fire from burning them all to cinders. He had to know Elice was well.

Plate still in hand, Adar crossed the courtyard and stepped past the doors to a round room lit with lamps and filled to the brim with books and tables for the historians. He and his father loved this tower. To Adar's left, two guards stood beside the stairs, wearing his mother's blasted sun emblem. He strode to-ward the stairs without hesitation.

The guards exchanged glances. As they stepped to block him, one of the men said, "Prince Adar, your mother has ex-pressly forbidden your entrance."

Fire and burning! Adar let the fire lick up first one arm and then another. "To be clear, neither of you can stop me."

The man on the right, the one who had spoken, opened and closed his hands around his spear. "My prince, please, we—"

"I'm not in a mood to negotiate." The fire started at the nape of Adar's neck and flared up his head, but it did not burn his hair or his skin. The flames never burned anything unless he wanted them to.

Again the guards glanced anxiously at each other. "You know we have to tell her," said the one on the left.

They always did. He pushed the plate of leftovers into one guard's hands. "Enjoy."

He pushed past them. At a dozen steps up, he laid down a blanket of fire so the guards couldn't follow. He tied the connection to summer, ensuring the flames wouldn't dissipate. Then he jogged up the stairs. He was no longer used to the oppressive heat. The air felt hot and heavy in his lungs, and his robes were soaked with sweat by the time he reached the top of the tower.

Beyond an ornate door was the head historian's quarters. Adar had been here many times with his father. The old historian, Baleesh, must have been moved to other rooms in the palace. Adar pushed on the door, which swung soundlessly open. Inside was another circular room lined with books. Chairs of dark wood surrounded a large table. The room was divided in half by a bookcase with another door in the center.

Adar strode to the door and push it open slightly. He could just make out Elice lying on her back on a wide bed. She had dark circles under her eyes, and her face seemed unnaturally pale in the candlelight. Beside the bed stood Adar's mother and Jezzel, their backs to him.

"Yes," Nelay said in a hushed tone. "I'll admit she was not what I expected."

Jezzel chuckled. "You mean because she was supposed to be forty years old, and instead she's young and beautiful?"

Nelay huffed and sat in a chair beside the bed. Her position gave Adar a clear shot of her face. "Leto must have given the elice blossom to Ilyenna, who in turn gave it to her husband and daughter. It's why she hasn't aged." Obviously tired, Nelay rubbed her face. "The look on Adar's face when he spoke of this girl . . . he's grown attached to her."

Jezzel gave a sharp intake of breath. "You don't think he has feelings for her?"

Adar cursed himself. That flare of fire on his arm must have given him away.

"He has an unfortunate propensity to"—his mother paused as if searching for the right word—"champion those far beneath himself, so I'm not sure how deep his feelings run. But it won't be long before we find out."

His mother had always seen his compassion as a weakness, while Adar considered it a strength.

Frowning, Jezzel dragged a chair close to Nelay's. "So what's your plan now?"

Nelay stared at Elice, whose face was serene and beautiful. She looked innocent and fresh as new-fallen snow. "I know Ilyenna too well," Nelay went on. "If she believes we mean the girl harm, she will come."

Jezzel gasped. "You mean to torture her?"

Adar clenched his jaw to keep silent. His mother had sworn to him that she would not harm Elice.

"I mean to execute her in three days unless Ilyenna agrees to my terms."

Adar's hands itched for his swords, and he nearly bolted into the room. He would not allow this. He would die before he allowed this.

"But that is murder," Jezzel said in shock.

Nelay went to Elice's side and brushed the back of her fingers across the princess's soft cheek. "One small evil done to stop a larger one. The life of this one girl could stop this war, Jezzel."

"Kill her and you lose any leverage you might have had with her mother," Jezzel pointed out.

"If Ilyenna won't agree to peace to save her daughter's life, Elice is of no value to us."

Jezzel placed her hands protectively around her belly. "You promised Adar you wouldn't hurt her. It's the only reason he agreed to help you in the first place."

"I don't have a choice."

"You always have a choice." When Nelay didn't respond, Jezzel pushed herself to her feet. "I won't be a part of this. And neither can you, Nelay. It will leave a stain on your soul you will never be free of."

His mother lifted a strand of Elice's thick black hair and rolled it between her fingers. "You're assuming I have a soul—that it was not burned away the day the fairies took me."

There was another long silence before Jezzel spoke. "I won't stand by and watch you do this."

"Are you threatening me?" Nelay asked softly.

Jezzel chuckled bitterly. "No, but I will take my family and go."

Nelay dropped Elice's hair and turned to her friend. "After all we have faced together, you would leave me over this girl?" The two traded glares. "Go back to your rooms, Jez. We'll talk about this again tomorrow."

Adar backed away from the door and silently lifted a chair away from the table. He grabbed an open book, propped his feet up, and, after making sure the book wasn't upside down, pretended to be reading. His mother and Jezzel came out a moment later. He didn't acknowledge them, simply kept reading without actually understanding any of the words.

"Adar?" His mother's voice was low and full of warning.

He held up a finger, as if he couldn't be bothered to stop reading.

"My guards?" his mother said darkly.

Knowing much depended on his performance, Adar shrugged. "I told them they could stand down or die. They decided to depend on your mercy."

"So much determination," Nelay mocked.

He set the book down carefully, feigning concern about losing his place, then folded his hands across his middle. "So this is where you're keeping her. What did you do with Master Baleesh?"

His mother glanced behind Jezzel, into the room where Elice was being held. "I bribed him with books from your father's personal collection."

That would do it. The love of Baleesh's life was books, his children their stories.

Jezzel crossed the room and pulled out a chair, then straddled it to face Adar with her arms crossed over the back of it. "How much did you hear?"

He ignored the question. "Elice is *my* prisoner, Mother. I have a right to know where she's being kept."

Nelay's gaze hardened. "If you can't live with this, I'll take Elice elsewhere. It's not like you can stop me."

The same threat Adar had leveled at the guards—and equally as true. A shot of fear pierced him to the core, and he struggled to keep his expression blank. Scrambling for a way to keep Elice safe, he realized he would have to reveal some of his secrets. But his plan might backfire.

Adar pushed from his chair and strode toward the room where Elice lay, his eyes daring his mother to try to stop him. To his relief, she stepped aside. He stopped next to the bed. Elice's beauty made his breath catch in his throat. She had been bathed and then dressed in a simple, long cotton nightgown. Her curly hair flared on the pillow behind her head. Her breaths sounded deep and even, as if she were merely sleeping.

"When will Tix's venom wear off?" Adar asked.

"Sometime tomorrow," his mother said.

He sank to his knees next to Elice and took her hand in both of his. With his thumbs, he traced the veins on the back of her hand. "I'm sorry," he whispered. "If I could drown myself in those dark waters before you ever saw me, I would do it." But the words were too little and too late. And now he was going to have to keep her safe as she'd kept him safe.

With an effort of will, Adar turned back to his mother, who watched him as if he'd just confirmed something she'd suspected.

"Fool boy," Jezzel said from beside her. "You fell in love with your enemy." She was nothing if not blunt.

"Doesn't it bother you that Nagale lied to us about the princess?" Adar asked.

Nelay grunted. "She'll be dealt with. The real question is *why* she lied to us."

Adar didn't care about the why. Those lies had cost him everything he'd never known he wanted. His gaze didn't waver from Nelay's. "Elice isn't her mother. She's the most gentle, determined girl I have ever met. I betrayed her, and she will hate me for it. But I will see that she is safe and cared for."

His mother's chin came up. "So you heard everything."

"Harm her and I swear I'll go to war with you myself."

"Don't threaten me!" Nelay's wings rolled from her back with a blast of heat.

Jezzel yelped and rushed out of the room. Adar stood protectively before Elice. His mother's heat couldn't hurt him any more than winter hurt Elice. But it *could* burn this tower down. As if to warn both Adar and his mother, a green tincture in a vial on the table began to boil.

Nelay stormed toward the balcony, threw open the double doors, and stepped outside. The heat from her wings dissipated in the night sky. "You and Jezzel take the moral high ground while I do what must be done alone," said the Summer Queen. "Well, when the world is finally at peace, we'll see who saved it." She spread her wings.

"I love her, Mother," Adar called out. "I would marry her tonight if she would agree."

Nelay froze and turned back to him, the heat from her wings distorting her face. "What would you have me do? Let this weapon sit, unused, while the War of the Queens rages on? How many more must die in the name of your love?"

"Please." He was not above begging. Not for this. Yet he saw it would not sway his mother. "A bargain then."

His mother's head came up. She was a fairy, after all, and no fairy could resist a bargain. "Adar, you know better than anyone that when a mortal makes a deal with a fairy, the mortal always loses." Even as Nelay warned him, her eyes sparked with hunger.

"I know," Adar ground out.

"What do you want, my son?"

He tipped his head toward Elice. "Her."

"Does she want you after what you've done?"

He didn't know the answer to that.

Nelay's expression turned calculating. "Very well. I will grant your request. You can have Elice. For three days. By the end of those three days, she must declare that she loves you— and she must mean it. If she does, she lives. If she does not, I will deliver the killing blow myself. If she discovers this bargain before it is through, I win. Do you agree?"

"And your price?" Adar asked softly.

His mother cocked her head to the side. "A life for a life."

He felt the blood drain from his face. "My life?"

"It is the price the Balance demands."

Adar knew his mother's humanity had been burned from her the day she became queen. But she'd always acted out of love, even though she might not feel the emotion. Still, he'd never thought his mother would require this of him, her firstborn son.

Jezzel stepped cautiously into the room, a sheen of perspiration on her face. "Adar, she may be your mother, but she's a Goddess of Fire first," warned Nelay's friend. "She won't spare you from the price, not in a bargain."

Adar ignored her. He'd stolen Elice's life, and if this was the way to give it back to her, so be it. "You will allow me whatever methods I require to regain her trust?"

His mother raised an eyebrow. "As long as your methods do not put you within reach of the Winter Queen."

"Then I agree." He felt the bands of the bargain snap into place, sealing around him. Nothing he or anyone else did would ever let him escape.

"Fool boy," Jezzel growled.

"Adar, the next time you intimidate my guards into disobeying me, I'll kill them for not stopping you. Jezzel, see my son out." Nelay soared into the sky and within seconds was out of sight.

Adar closed his eyes. "Jezzel, you have to stop her."

"Short of killing her, how do you expect me to do that?" He winced, and Jezzel rested her hand on her enormous belly. "She's not fully human, Adar. Not anymore. You need to remember that."

He shook his head, hating that his mother's friend was right. He moved to the bed and sat beside Elice, not sure he was strong enough to walk away from her now. "Let me stay."

"After what you did, Elice won't thank you for the company," Jezzel reminded him.

Adar took Elice's hand, which felt as small and fragile as a fallen dove. "She shouldn't be alone."

He heard Jezzel move to stand next to him. "But she is alone. She's the enemy and our captive. That's the very definition of alone."

I did this to her. Adar swallowed hard. Elice needed someone. Someone like her, to help her through this. Someone who would be loyal to him. Someone who owed him her life. "Cinder."

Jezzel's head came up. "The queen's dressmaker?"

He nodded. "Her mother was a clanwoman." Cinder owed Adar her life. And he trusted her.

Jezzel slowly nodded and then headed for the door. "I'll see she's sent for."

"By the fairies," Adar said.

She hesitated at the threshold before repeating, "By the fairies." She paused. "Adar, it's time to go."

"Please . . . just a moment?"

Jezzel sighed heavily and shut the door behind her.

Adar knelt beside Elice's bed. "I will keep you safe, Elice." Unable to resist, he leaned forward and pressed a soft kiss against the back of her hand, which felt cool even in the sweltering heat of the Idaran summer night. "I swear it on my life."

At the observation tower, Adar waited with his arms crossed, staring blindly over the Adrack Desert. The wind picked up, shifting his wide pants against his legs and wicking the sweat from his bare chest. The heaviness of the air shocked him. Months in the Winter Queendom had left his skin dry and cracking, but now the humidity of early spring felt like a living thing, suffocating and heavy.

He had appreciated the warmth afforded by his long hair in the frozen wasteland of the Winter Queendom. But now it was hot and sticky. He lit up his head, using the summer wind to blow the ashes off before they could stick to his sweaty shoulders. He ran his hands over his now-bald head, wondering what Elice would think of the thick tattoos crossing his scalp.

Then his thoughts circled around to the price of the bargain. He or Elice would die. Fire and burning, there had to be another way.

"This was not the plan, dearest prince."

Adar spun around, his eyes catching on the gleaming towers—gold by day, silver by moonlight. On one of the railings crouched an owl with a fairy on its back. This fairy was withered, with only a few white and black feathers clinging to her diseased skin.

"You lied to me," Adar accused.

Nagale clacked her sharp beak at him. "I never lie."

His hand went to the shamshir at his waist. "Twisting the truth is still a lie."

Nagale chuckled, a sound that was anything but pleasant. "That is how the game is played. Lies mixed with truths, and manipulation mixed with betrayal."

Adar pulled the sword from its sheath. "The princess is my age! And she's not evil and twisted! You were supposed to see my ship safely to and from the Winter Palace, but it sank, killing everyone on board. I nearly died half a dozen times. You lied to me about everything!" He never should have trusted Nagale. He should have known everything would end up twisted. That he would lose more than he was willing to pay.

"We will all die. That's the point," Nagale suddenly shouted, angry and half mad. "But that doesn't mean I lied." Now her voice turned sing-song. It seemed that whatever corruption had destroyed her body had also destroyed her mind. "Do you love her?"

Adar shifted to a defensive stance. "What?"

"Do you love her?"

He took a step back, not wanting this creature to know the truth.

"Answer me honestly, prince."

He held out his arms helplessly to his side. "I was supposed to bring her safely here. That was our bargain. That was your price for helping us save the world."

The fairy's yellow eyes, huge in her sunken face, regarded him coolly. "Does the princess return your love?"

Adar exhaled loudly. "If she ever did, she doesn't anymore."

Nagale twisted her head to look out over the desert. "Bargains," she cackled as the owl spread its white wings. "Only the truly desperate make them. Only the truly desperate need them. And always, the desperate pay."

As Adar watched Nagale fly away, his fist clenched around his sword so hard he could feel each ridge of the grip leaving an imprint on his hand.

"Adar?"

He spun, sword arching, and only managed to pull the swing at the last second. Cinder stumbled away from him, falling to the ground in a flutter of silks. She cursed him as only the daughter of a prostitute could. He held out a hand to her. She glared up at him, then ruefully took it.

"Idiot Idaran!" She smoothed her silk robes and flipped her long hair over her shoulder. Her locks shone silver in the moonlight. "Why was I brought here in a huge net carried by all manner of blurs that sometimes looked like birds or insects, but more often than not had teeth and scales and stingers?" Cinder shuddered, her hand over her stomach. "You know how much I hate fairies."

Adar shoved his sword in its sheath and helped her to her feet. "Because I think you're the only one who can help me."

"You brought me all the way here to design some clothes for you?" She surveyed him, then waved mockingly at his bare chest. "Personally, I see no need to cover *that* up. I'm sure all the women of Idara would agree."

He rolled his eyes. "Cinder, I don't want you to make me any clothes. I brought you here to help her."

"Help who? And how?"

Adar took hold of Cinder's arm and started down the stairs. "Her name is Elice. I betrayed her—fire and burning, I didn't mean to, but I did all the same. But I might just be able to save her. If I can accomplish nothing else in my life, that alone will be worth it."

Cinder looked at him suspiciously. "Adar, have you been drinking?"

He tried to run his fingers through his hair before remembering he'd burned it all off. "I need your help."

Cinder squared her shoulders. "You point me to your enemy, and I'll kick their teeth in."

Suddenly Adar felt lighter. This burden wasn't just his anymore. And with Cinder by his side, there wasn't much he couldn't accomplish.

The venom slogged through Elice's body. Her eyelids felt so heavy. Fighting the poison, she struggled to wake herself. She was conscious of the slippery sheets that had bunched between her legs as she tossed. After what seemed like forever, she managed to open her eyes. Afraid of falling asleep again, she pushed herself up, feeling ragged and sore instead of rested. Dim light streamed through the windows. It was either very early in the morning or very late at night. She gaped at her surroundings—a lavish room with curving walls of stone, a turquoise-and-gold mosaic of tiles swirling on the ceiling above her. This was far from the dank dungeon she'd expected to find herself in.

She hauled herself to the edge of the enormous bed, the lilac sheets ensnaring her legs. She finally managed to free herself and simply sat, waiting for the world to stop spinning. She was wearing a thin cotton shift that was damp and crumpled, and her hair had been washed and combed. With some disquiet, Elice wondered who had done such a thing, but she pushed the worry from her mind. She had bigger problems.

There were three doors—one, a double-glass door that seemed to lead to a balcony. She struggled to her feet and moved to the door, swaying unsteadily as she went, but it was locked fast. She looked through it at the world outside and gasped in shock. A golden city sprawled out before her, all onion domes and ochre desert for as far as she could see. To her right, a glorious palace sat proudly inside a high wall and another courtyard, where fountains shot jets toward the cerulean sky. Channels had been built on tripods, but Elice couldn't guess the purpose for them. She could just make out people, all with dark hair and brilliantly colored robes, moving about both courtyards.

"There's so much color," she murmured.

Reminding herself that she had to escape, Elice spread her fingers on the windowpane and opened herself to winter, determined to break the glass and make her escape. But only the barest trickle streamed from her fingers, spreading ferns of frost across the smooth pane. She tried again, and more frost spread. Breathing hard, she yanked back her hand, staring at the imprint she'd left behind.

She closed her eyes and concentrated, pulling with everything she had. She managed to form a dagger, but it was so thin it shattered at the slightest pressure. She couldn't have even scratched someone with it. Without winter, she was practically powerless.

Again she looked out the door. Her mother had been right. Elice had won her freedom, but it had cost her everything. Her innocence, her magic, her family, and the only true friend she'd ever known, when she'd been forced to leave Sakari behind. Elice had also lost a bond she thought might last forever. In the end, even the freedom she'd gained had been taken.

Filled with dread, she turned to face the room. With the many colors and foreign designs here, a part of her wanted nothing more than to study it, replicate it. But beautiful or not, this was her prison. She must find a way out.

Two sets of double doors carved from dark wood were framed within delicate arches that wore a fringe of lace-like stone. Elice moved to the partially open door and found a bathroom. After she had relieved herself, she drank deep from a water basin and then splashed some of the cool liquid on her face to wake herself up. There were dozens of bright-emerald bottles, which she was tempted to open.

But her dread at what awaited her propelled Elice to the third door. The water and the movement seemed to help with the grogginess, as she didn't stagger once. She pushed on the door, which opened easily at her touch.

This was some sort of receiving room, with a round table and chairs, shelves with wonderfully fat books, and heavy-looking rugs. But all of that was barely visible through the piles of fabrics in every hue Elice had ever dreamed of. She stepped forward as if in a dream and sank her fingers into the colors. She lifted the fabrics to her face and rubbed them against her cheek. The fabric felt soft and light as a breeze.

"I'm Cinder," a voice said.

Elice whirled around. On a balcony beyond another open door sat a woman of about thirty years. Her delicate hands made quick work with a bone needle. But it was the woman's face that caught Elice's attention, for it was a face that did not belong—not here. Her hair was blonde and curly, her skin pale and freckled. She had a curvier, shorter build than the tall, muscular women Elice had spied in the courtyard. And she was perhaps the most breathtakingly beautiful woman Elice had ever seen. Her eyes, the charcoal hue of storm clouds, were fixed on Elice.

Elice recognized her for what she was, because she'd seen the same traits all her life. "You're a clanwoman."

The woman paused, her fingers stilling. "My mother was. Unfortunately, I am Idaran."

"Are you my jailer?"

Cinder laughed. "No."

"My friend Sakari—is she all right?"

"I don't know."

Elice gave a little huff. "Is it morning or night?"

"Very early morning. But a very late night for me. I only arrived a few hours ago, and they said you should be waking soon. So I waited." The woman went back to her work, picking up right where she'd left off. "I've been commissioned to make your clothes. You should be flattered—new clients usually have to wait a few years."

Elice watched as the needle pierced the delicate fabric again and again. "I don't understand why I'm here."

"No," Cinder sighed. "I suppose you don't. I don't understand it myself. Not really." She gathered the fabric, then rose and entered the room. With the light coming in from behind her, her face was cast in shadows. "You've been asleep for three days. He sent me to be here when you woke up. He thought a woman who spoke your language, who looked like you, who loved other clanwomen, would be a comfort to you. It's why I agreed to come from the Adrack."

"He?"

Cinder cocked her head. "Don't you know?"

Elice turned away, angry. She did know—Adar. "Why am I here instead of a dungeon?"

"You are a princess, are you not?"

"No," Elice answered darkly. "My mother is a queen, but I am not her heir."

"Aren't you?" Cinder approached the table, set down whatever she was making, and dug around in the fabric until she produced a covered tray. She opened it without another word, revealing crackers, cheese, and some water. She pulled out a chair and motioned for Elice to sit.

The smell of the salty cheese hit her then, and her stomach clenched with sickness. With her hand over her mouth, Elice took a step back. Cinder quickly covered the tray. "They said you might be queasy. It will pass."

Cinder picked up the garment she'd been working on and held the snow-white fabric to Elice, who pushed it away. She'd been surrounded by white her entire life. Undeterred, Cinder went back to work. "You will wear this when you meet with the Goddess of Summer in a few days. I didn't have time to make it from scratch. Luckily at my shop in the city we have many garments already sewn. I simply made a few adjustments and added some flare. You'll look like a princess, I swear it."

Elice opened her mouth to make it clear how much she hated white, but then hesitated. She was of the Winter Queendom. Her mother was the queen. Elice had turned her back on that once, and look where it had landed her.

"White and silver," she finally agreed. "Winter's colors."

Cinder nodded in approval. "White yes, but not silver—it's not in your color pallet. Gold is." Elice didn't argue, since she'd always loved gold more than silver. Cinder had her stand as she draped the dress over her shoulders. "I measured you while you slept, so of course it will fit. I just wanted to check how it drapes."

Immediately Elice recognized the style, and tears stung her eyes. It was clannish clothing—an overdress with an underdress. She'd even be able to wear her clan belt with it. "What are they going to do with me?"

"In three days, you are to have an audience with the queen and be presented to the lords and ladies of Idara."

A wave of dread nearly swept Elice's feet out from under her. "For what purpose?"

"Adar is on your side," Cinder said quietly. "He's been plotting and planning since he arrived. No one does it better than him, except perhaps his mother."

"I've seen that firsthand. Whose side are you on?"

Cinder's fingers paused before resuming their work. "I know what it is to be trapped. That, perhaps more than my skill, is why Adar sent for me. And why I agreed to come back."

"Come back?"

Cinder's eyes flashed like a storm building over a boiling sea. "I hate Idara."

"I know what it is to hate your heritage." Elice glanced back at the pale-blue sky, at the light streaming through the window and catching on motes of dust—without the snow to cover the ground, the air must be choked with it. "Are you loyal to Nelay?"

"They are always listening." Cinder swung out the dress, which flared and floated as she settled it on some sort of fabric dress form and began making adjustments. Elice's hope flared, then faltered just as quickly. Perhaps Cinder really would try to help her, but what match was a seamstress against a Summer Queen?

"Adar wants you to look like a princess when they present you to the crowd, and so you shall."

Cinder led Elice to the bathroom and showed her how to work the faucet. "It's cold," she said with a shrug, "but then you learn to appreciate anything cold in the desert."

Elice was already stripping out of her soiled shift. Her skin felt oddly damp and uncomfortable. "The cold has never harmed me."

"I suppose not," Cinder answered as she laid an underdress on a long table. "I still have a few adjustments to make on your overdress, so take your time."

Sinking into the cool water was a relief. With her discomfort lessened, Elice soon discovered that each soap had a scent, so she used them all. When she stepped out, water dripping from her skin, she paused before the emerald bottles. Then she reached out and grasped one. Beneath the pads of her fingers, the glass felt as hard and slick as ice, sending a pang of homesickness through her. She uncorked the lid and was inundated with a floral scent. She tried another and another. Rich spicy scents, warm muted scents, sweet and light scents. Elice chose a sweet and spicy fragrance. The oil pooled across her palm and made her hands slip over her skin.

She donned the underdress and stepped into the bedroom to see the wind howling past the patio doors, churning up great masses of tan-colored dirt. She pressed her forehead to the glass but could see only a few people. They wore veils over their faces and hair, so just their eyes and hands showed. Bits of dust had gathered at the corners of the doors, spilling into the room like snow from the Winter Queen's blizzards.

"It's like this every afternoon and evening. It will be over soon," Cinder said from behind Elice.

Feeling lethargic and uncomfortable, Elice wiped away the moisture on her forehead. "What will?"

"The sand storm. The one in the afternoon is the ovat. The one in the evening is the tavo." Cinder came to stand beside her.

More moisture trickled down Elice's back. "Why am I wet?" she muttered. "I've dried myself off." Cinder shot her a confused look. Elice wiped her brow, which was damp again, and showed the other woman the moisture on her fingers as proof.

Understanding dawned on Cinder's face. "It's sweat—your body makes moisture on your skin to cool you when it's hot. You've really never sweated before?"

Elice blinked. She was going to be uncomfortable and . . . sweaty, the whole time she was in Thanjavar? "It never gets above freezing in the queendom. Even if it did, my magic rages through me—or it used to." Sick with all that she had lost, she looked back out the window. "Is it always this . . . hot?"

"Always." Cinder shrugged. "You sort of get used to it." She shook herself and pulled out the overdress she'd been cradling in her arms. It was a saturated coral, with pleated folds of linen draping handsomely. But what thrilled Elice more than anything was the style of the clothing—distinctly clannish.

"Oh, thank you," she breathed.

Cinder smiled. "I'll have more made. If you're going to be here, you'll look like the princess you are."

Elice pulled the overdress over her head, then tied her gold clan belt across her waist. Cinder parted Elice's hair, braided it, and tied it off with a simple ribbon.

When Cinder finished, Elice felt more like herself again. Unable to help herself, she gathered the other woman in her arms. "Thank you."

Cinder patted her awkwardly on the back. "So you're pleased?"

"Oh yes. I've never worn such beautiful garments before—and in such bright colors!"

Cinder took a few steps back, toward the door. "Pleased enough to promise not to be angry?"

Elice's smile fell. "Why?"

Cinder simply opened the door and stepped into the main room. Elice hesitated, suddenly loath to follow, but forced herself through the doorway. What she saw made her stop in her tracks.

Relief washed through Adar to see Elice up and moving. But he didn't dare approach her. Not yet. "Cinder told me you were asking about Sakari," he said to her. "I wanted you to know she's all right. I made sure of it before I left."

Elice's eyes fluttered closed in relief, but then she said through clenched teeth, "Get out."

"Elly, let me explain."

"Get out!" She picked up a book from the shelf and hurled it at him. He wasn't prepared for it and it hit him on his newly healed shoulder, sending a pulse of fresh pain through the joint. "Not the books, Elly!"

She sent another one flying. This one, Adar ducked. "Don't you dare call me Elly! My family and friends call me that—not you!"

"Just let me explain—"

With an enormous tome in hand, she marched toward him. He backed toward the door, hands up. "Elly—Elice, I don't blame you for being angry, but—"

"I never want to see you again." She wound up and flung the book at him.

Bracing himself, Adar ducked so that the blow hit his upper arm instead of his head. "Don't hit me again," he warned.

She glared at him, panting. "I hate you."

"You think I wanted this? You think I wanted to fall in love with the woman I was supposed to deceive? It's not fair, to either of us—"

Elice's fist shot out, but he sidestepped the blow, took her arm, and jerked her forward, then used his leg to trip her. But she twisted out of it and hooked her elbow into Adar's back. He pivoted and wrapped an arm around her to take her to the floor. She started to scramble out of his hold. He shifted, gripping her tight. Elice was good, but out of practice, which was fortunate, because she'd very nearly had him.

"I had my reasons," he panted. "If you'd just listen."

She struggled against him. "There's never a good reason to trick someone into falling in love with you."

"I didn't trick—"

She threw her elbow back, hitting him between the legs. All the breath was forced from his lungs. White-hot waves of pain shot upward until he thought he would vomit. He broke out in a sweat. A moan escaped him as he curled into a ball. Hearing Elice scramble up to stand over him, he imagined her fierce expression. For a moment, he wondered if she would kill him.

Cinder inserted herself between them. "Adar, get out."

"I'm never . . . going to be able to have children," he managed.

Not taking her eyes off Elice, Cinder bent down and helped him up. "Go."

Sucking in a breath, he staggered to the door. He pulled it open and stepped out, wanting to slam it behind him, but unable to use that much force. Then he sagged against the wall, waiting for the pain and dizziness to recede enough that he could move down the blasted stairs. Next time he wouldn't ditch the guards his mother had insisted on.

When he heard the soft sounds of weeping from the other side of the door, Adar's anger melted away. His eyes slipped closed. If she wouldn't even speak to him, how was he supposed to get her to declare her love for him? How could he possibly get her out of here alive?

His gut wrenched. Elice was going to die. And it was all his fault. Moving gingerly, he made his way down the stairs and behind the palace. Waves of pain still swept from his crotch up his abdomen, but it wasn't as sharp. Wishing for some of the ice from the winter queendom, he stood at the edge of the fountain and stared out over the city, trying to think of something, anything that would save Elice.

He wasn't sure how long he stood there before he realized he was being watched. As if sensing she'd been noticed, one of his younger sisters stepped into view. Carrying their youngest sibling, their sister Mahin, on her hip, Zahra wore a long robe and veil, so only her eyes showed. Eyes that brimmed with tears she angrily blinked back. "You're home and you didn't even come to see me?"

Adar let out a defeated sigh. "I can't seem to do anything right, Zahra."

More of his siblings popped into view. The boys, Navid and Omid, reached him first. They swarmed him, hugging and tugging and jostling and speaking all at once. The girls, Yasmin and Laleh, were a beat behind. Hunched protectively around his injury, Adar hugged them carefully.

"Where is everyone else?" he asked.

"Javed, Roshan, and Bahadur are at weapons practice. Father said I can start practicing with them this winter," Navid declared proudly, while Omid turned sullen.

"Nahid, Parvaneh, and Shirin said if you wanted to see them, you had to come to the palace to do it," Zahra grumbled.

She marched toward Adar. He reached for Mahin, but she shrank away from him. Had his baby sister forgotten him already? Zahra angled her body so she was between him and the baby. "When the other ship came back without you, I was sure you were dead—we all were." She said the last bit with a betrayed glare at their siblings—probably for betraying her anger by hugging him. "Then I heard you'd been found and were coming home. You didn't even bother to come see me. To see any of us. We've been searching for you all day."

"I'm sorry, it's just . . ." Adar stared at his feet. "You know the girl I was supposed to bring back?"

"The winter princess," Nahid said with round eyes.

Yasmin shuddered. "Was she horrible and ugly?"

Adar gave them a stern look. "She isn't anything like we thought. She's beautiful and smart and kind and . . ." *She's going to die*, he finished in his head, reminding himself that Zahra, at thirteen, was the oldest.

Zahra moved slowly toward him. "You like her?"

"Why would you like her?" Javed asked. "Her mother killed half of our countrymen."

Adar sighed. "But Elice didn't. She was only a baby like Mahin when that happened." His gaze went back to Zahra. "She's very angry that I tricked her into coming here."

Zahra studied him with a gaze that seemed much older than her years. "So apologize."

"I tried. She won't listen to me."

"Give her some time."

Adar shook his head. "I don't have time."

"It's not like she's going anywhere," Zahra said dryly.

Adar choked, fighting back the despair. "I made a deal with Mother."

Zahra's eyes widened. She turned to their siblings and handed Mahin to Nahid. "All of you head back to the palace."

Nahid gaped at Adar. "Why would you make a deal with her?" Like Zahra, Nahid was old enough to understand what Adar had done.

Before Adar could answer, Zahra started shooing their young brothers and sisters toward the palace. "Move it. Go!" When they'd finally scampered off, she whirled around and punched Adar in the arm. "You know better than to make deals with fairies."

"I had no choice. Elice has three days to admit she's in love with me. That's the bargain I made. It was the best I could do to save her life."

"You fell in love with her," Zahra gasped.

Miserable, Adar dropped his head. "I couldn't help it. It just happened."

"Does she love you back?"

He took a long breath and let it out slowly. "I think she might have."

"Would seeing me—would that change her mind?" Zahra whispered after moving a step closer.

"It might."

"Take me to her."

Adar stared at his sister. If Elice could see what the Sundering had done to Zahra, maybe she would believe him. But he knew what this would cost his sister. "Zahra, are you sure?"

She gave a determined smile. "It's not like I haven't endured worse."

At the sound of voices in the other room, Elice left the bland food she'd been picking and tiptoed to the door.

"I don't think she's ready." It was Cinder's voice.

"There isn't time for her to be ready."

Adar was back so soon? Elice balled her hands into fists. It had been very satisfying to hit him. She wouldn't mind doing it again.

"Adar . . ."

"I only have three days, Cinder."

Three days for what? Elice wondered. A beat of silence, and then footsteps moved toward the door. She stepped back, arms crossed over her stomach. Cinder slipped inside and shut the door behind her.

"I won't talk to him," Elice told her.

Cinder leaned against the closed door. "I think you should."

Elice shot her a glare. "Why?"

"Because he'll keep coming back until he says whatever it is he needs to say. The sooner you get it over with, the sooner you can be done."

Elice considered for a moment. Then she sighed and reached around Cinder to jerk open the door. "I told you, I—" The words choked in her throat. Adar wasn't alone. There was someone with him, a small person partially hidden behind him as if afraid of Elice. In addition, a pair of guards stood farther back.

Adar leaned toward the other person and said, "This is the girl I was telling you about."

The person straightened and came out from behind him. "My name is Zahra," she said with a slight lisp. Judging by her voice and slight build, she was a young girl. She was covered from head to toe in fine linen, with only her eyes revealed. She took another step forward. "I want to show you something."

Elice worked her tongue inside her dry mouth and shifted her gaze to Adar. "What kind of trick is this?"

"It's not a trick," Zahra answered.

Elice's gaze settled on the girl. "I don't want anything to do with him."

"He'll leave as soon as you promise not to hurt me or run away," Zahra said.

Elice gritted her teeth, disgusted that Adar would use a child as a go-between. "Will he promise to leave me alone after this?"

Zahra sent Adar a questioning look, but his gaze was pinned on Elice. "If you refuse to see me after this, I'll stay away," he said.

Elice considered for a moment. "Then I promise to behave."

Adar turned and left without another word. Elice found herself glaring at his retreating figure and feeling darkly satisfied at how stiffly he moved. Cinder stepped up beside Elice and said softly, "She's a sweet girl—only thirteen—and she's been through a lot. Be kind to her."

Zahra motioned for Elice to follow her. An unreasonable fear pulsed through Elice, causing her to hesitate before moving to obey. Beyond the door, she was still surrounded by books. She stepped out to find stairs spiraling down, down, down. She stepped carefully to the edge and saw a long drop that ended in a hard stone floor. She stepped back, her arm coming up against the cool stone walls.

Zahra watched her, sympathy in her gaze. "Stick to the outside and you'll be fine."

Straightening her shoulders, Elice picked up her dress and started down the stairs, staying exactly in the middle to show the other girl she wasn't afraid. At the bottom of the stairs stood two guards. They didn't acknowledge Elice and Zahra as they passed, but Elice felt their eyes on her.

She found herself in a round room with a mosaic floor of a phoenix rising from the ashes. There were more books—hundreds of them—and long tables littered with lamps that looked like slender, long teapots, with flames sputtering out instead of tea.

Zahra stepped up beside her. "This way."

Elice glanced back at the two guards trailing behind. She hurried to catch up to Zahra. They stepped past an intricately carved door—mermaids in a churning sea. The sunlight blinded Elice and she squinted, her hand automatically rising to shield her eyes. She gazed up toward the sun and blinked. Though she couldn't look at it directly, it was obviously much bigger than in the queendom. And far too high in the sky. Elice could feel the heat baking her skin, seeping into her pores. She took another step forward and was shocked to feel the heat burning through the soles of her sandals.

Before her loomed the palace, a monstrous structure with lacy arches and golden onion domes. Without the power of winter, Elice couldn't imagine how many years it had taken to construct. Zahra was waiting patiently a few steps ahead. "My brother wanted me to warn you that if you run, you will be bound from here on out. He also said"—Zahra's eyes scrunched up as if she were remembering—"that the queen's fairies are always watching."

Lips pressed in a thin line, Elice caught up with the girl. The dry air caught in her throat, making her cough and wish for a drink. They bypassed the front of the main gate that led to the palace's wide stairs and ornate entrance, and headed for another set of shorter walls with wide-open gates. "This is the temple of the Goddess of Fire. It's older than the palace. Thanjavar is our holy city."

"The city where the War of the Queens started," Elice said, recalling the stories Chriel had told her.

Zahra paused. "Yes. And by the Balance, where it ends."

Side by side the two young women crossed the gates. Many geometrically shaped fountains decorated the courtyard. People surrounded them, placing something burning in the ashy water. Elice looked closer and saw shapes—seagulls and lions and even a mouse, all made of folds of paper. The air was sharp with a sweet-smelling smoke.

"Why are they burning them?"

"So their prayers will be carried up by the smoke," Zahra answered.

She and Elice passed through ornate pillars into a cool, cavernous room. There was another enormous pool, the still water dotted with floating, burning paper. An enormous glass idol of a winged woman stood in the center, smoke seeping through the tendrils of her hair. Elice watched in fascination as money was exchanged for paper written on before being twisted and folded into intricate shapes by young girls with quick fingers.

Zahra and Elice passed another set of stunningly muscled guards and entered a large corridor, their steps echoing off the stone walls. It was cooler here and closed off. The turned left and passed smaller rooms with private pools, and smaller glass idols with curling smoke inside. Elice and Zahra came out into another room that mirrored the first, only with golden columns surrounded by rings of oil, burning wicks trailing out of them. Women of all ages knelt on prayer cushions. Zahra passed everything as if she'd seen such amazing sights every day of her life. Perhaps she had.

"What is all this?" Elice asked.

"The Temple of Fire," the girl answered. "It's where the priestesses are trained. We write the people's prayers on paper soaked in incense. We worship the Goddess of Fire."

"You mean the Summer Queen," Elice said darkly.

Zahra shrugged. "That's what you call her."

They passed through the pivot doors and into another courtyard. On the opposite side was a long building with dozens of closely spaced doors. In the center of the courtyard was another fountain, this one with statues of naked girls frolicking in the water. Neat rows of trees marched up and down the courtyard. Along the left side were dozens of girls Zahra's age and younger, fighting with wooden swords.

Zahra paused, watching them intently. "They are the reason he came for you."

Elice shot her an uneasy glance before edging forward. As she came closer, she realized there was something very, very wrong with them. One girl had white feathers instead of hair.

Another had a golden mane and tail. Yet another had faceted insect eyes.

Breathing hard, Elice stumbled back. "They're fairies! They're all fairies." She bumped into Zahra and whirled around.

"No," Zahra answered. "It's the magic. My mother says it's sick, and the sickness is bleeding into those born with the Sight." Zahra unpinned her veil, revealing scaly skin that was fleshy colored except for a bright red flare at her throat. There were spikes on the side of her neck, with toothlike, downward-curving horns growing from her jaw. "Girls like me." When she spoke, her mouth was black and fanged and her tongue was long and slitted—that explained the lisp.

Elice stumbled back. "Your mother?"

"The Goddess of Fire, Nelay. Adar is my brother."

Elice had to close her eyes so she could talk to the girl without screaming. "Are you like them—like the fairies?"

Zahra sighed. "That's why I wear the veil, so people don't look at me the way you just did."

Elice felt a surge of guilt and forced herself to open her eyes. After the initial shock and rush of instinctual fear, she realized the girl was just a girl.

"It started a little over fourteen years ago," Zahra went on. "I was one of the first born like this. I was lucky—my mother's status protects me. Not so for the others. Some were killed at birth by their parents or the midwives. Others were named fairy spawn and burned at the temples by terrified citizens. My mother put a stop to it. All the girls come here now. When we go out, we stay fully covered. Only here, behind the temple, do we reveal ourselves."

"I'm sorry," Elice whispered.

"It's not all bad. I can sense heat." The girl pointed to pits on her neck and jaw. "You're colder than anything else here, like a snake on a cold morning."

Elice swallowed hard. "Why did this happen to you?"

"Because of the Sundering. Adar promised he would find a way to stop it. That's why he sailed to your queendom. That's why he brought you here."

"But he still tricked me . . . lied to me."

Zahra's expression softened. "Don't the clanmen having a saying that sometimes you have to lose a lamb to save the flock? Something like that."

Elice had heard her grandfather say the exact thing when looking at a drawing of his daughter, her laughing expression, the joy in her eyes. Elice had never seen her mother like that. Never seen her smile so broadly it lit up her whole face. "I'm not a sheep."

Zahra studied her. "Which is why he's still trying to save you."

At the top of her tower, Elice stood at the open doorway. Adar sat at the table, a meal spread out before him. She looked him over, noting again how dangerous he looked with sharp, cutting tattoos replacing his soft curls. His hands were fisted on the table as if he expected her to attack.

But she didn't want to hurt him anymore. Now she only felt sadness and bitterness toward him. "Are you going to try again to convince me that the Sundering is real?"

Adar shook his head. "I figure you've had enough shocks for today."

Elice let out a silent sigh of relief. Any more revelations and she might shatter.

"Will you eat with me?" he finally asked.

She sighed and sat down opposite him. There were bowls of golden-yellow soup and a soft, fluffy lump. Both gave off delicious aromas that made Elice's mouth water. There were berries too—rich-red bumps in a cone shape. Adar had brought her the meal she'd told him about that day in the winter palace. Angry at the tears pricking her eyes, she forced herself to look away.

He picked up the white lump first. "This is called bread. It's made from a grain, which is a ground-up seed. It's soft in the middle and hard on the outside. I brought you some soft cheese to eat with it. There's also lamb stew. You told me once about how much your grandfather loved lamb stew. This one is probably different from what they make in the clanlands—they have different herbs. This is curry, and it's a little spicy. It's my favorite. And last, I bribed a fairy to give us some raspberries. I've never tried them either—it's too hot for them to grow here, and they're out of season anyway."

Elice wiped the tears from her cheeks and forced herself to be strong. "You're the enemy, Adar, so don't pretend to be my friend."

He took one of the bowls and sipped it, his eyes closing. "First, you taste the curry and the sweetness. A moment later, the lamb. Just when you think you've experienced everything, the spice heats up in your mouth."

Unable to look away, she watched him take the bread and break it in two. "This"—he shook his half at her—"is different from how we make it, but I convinced one of the cooks to try it the way your grandfather described." Adar laid a piece of cheese over the bread and took a bite. "It's not bad. A little dryer than our flatbread, but not bad." He dipped it in his soup and took another bite. "Oh, that's better."

Elice allowed herself a glance at the berries. Adar hadn't eaten one. She wondered what price he would pay, what precious thing he would give up, in exchange for them. She listened to the sounds of him eating, the way he described every bite—creamy and warm and sweet and savory. And she only grew angrier. "Do you think a few kindnesses will make up for your betrayal?"

Pain flashed across Adar's face. "I'm not asking you to forgive me. Just eat, you have to be hungry—you've barely eaten anything in three days. And then we'll talk."

Despite herself, Elice's stomach growled. The soup was just sitting there, growing cold. It would be a crime to waste it. Besides, she would need strength to make her escape. She reached out and took the bowl of soup, which was actually cool in her hands. She sipped it, and it was just like Adar described. She wasn't even sure she liked it—it was so different from the cold, raw meat she was used to. The spice took her by surprise, burning her mouth and making her eyes water.

She came across a piece of lamb, which was so different from fish. It was more like seal, only stringier and more flavorful. An orchestra played inside her mouth where there had only been a solo. Eagerly, she tried the bread, and the softness shocked her—the way it gummed up in her teeth. She dipped it in the soup and marveled at how something soggy could be so full of flavor.

Elice saved the berries for last. She rolled them gently around her fingers, noticing how the dozens of tiny globes had formed a soft cone. Unable to resist anymore, she popped a berry into her mouth. The tangy sweetness made her eyes flutter shut, and a little moan escaped her mouth. Embarrassed, she looked over the table to see if Adar had noticed.

He was watching her. Their eyes met, his silently begging for forgiveness. Something warm and soft spread between them. Elice turned away. She didn't want to care about him. She wanted to hate him. But her traitor heart wouldn't cooperate.

He strode to the other side of the table and picked up a pitcher that was sweating as hard as Elice. He poured thick white cream over the berries and then dusted them with crumbs of sugar. Though she had never seen anything like this, she'd heard her grandfather describe it enough times to know exactly what it was.

She didn't want to give Adar the satisfaction of knowing she enjoyed the berries, but she was far more afraid of letting this experience slip past her. After all, it would likely never come again. She filled her spoon with berries and cream and sugar. The first sensation was cold. Next came a sweet creaminess. Then Elice chewed and the sour exploded.

"They're opposites," she murmured. "That's why they complement each other so well—the sour with the creamy sweetness." Just like her art—hard with soft, round with sharp, and always in an unexpected way. She finished the bowl leisurely and then hesitated on the last berry, not wanting this moment to end.

"Elice, some things are going to happen," Adar began. "But you have to believe me when I tell you that no harm will come to you. I swear it by my own life."

She studied the remaining berry, watching as the cream was slowly stained purple and started to curdle. "When my mother comes . . ."

He opened his mouth to say something, then seemed to think better of it. Instead he explained, "Your mother would have almost no power in the Summer Realm. She would struggle just to fly. She won't come unless we force her hand."

Elice rolled the last berry under her spoon and squished it against the bowl until the juice leaked out. She scraped the ragged remains into her mouth and tried to lose herself in the flavor. But the sweetness was gone, leaving only the sour. "You brought me here so that Nelay could hurt my mother. I will never forgive you for that."

"You don't have to forgive me." Adar stood. "But I want you to understand why." He seemed sad as he said it.

Elice forced herself to meet his gaze. "Your sister and the other girls."

"Remember what I asked after we found that flooded village—what would you sacrifice to save the world? Do you remember what you said?"

She folded her arms across her chest, refusing to answer.

"That you didn't know. But I do. Because I've been faced with that choice, and I will live with the consequences of that decision." Adar sighed. "I managed to get permission to show you my home. Will you come?"

"Nelay trusts me that much?"

"You're no threat to us, Elice. Not so far from your powers."

She glared at him. "I am trained in the axe, bow, and dagger." But of course, she had no weapons. And in the Summer Realm, he didn't need weapons any more than she had needed them in the Winter Queendom.

Elice huffed and stood, then moved as far from him as possible. They were silent for a time, and she wondered when he'd finally leave her in peace. When Adar finally spoke, his voice almost startled her. "You've come all this way, and the Summer Realm waits just beyond the door. Will you not even see it?"

She wanted to say no, just like she'd wanted to say no to the food he had brought her. But all her life, she'd dreamed of seeing something outside the tiny confines of the queendom. The things she'd spent her whole life building replicas of in ice again and again and again. And besides, if there was a chance at escape, it would help if she knew the layout.

"What if we call a truce, just for a few hours each day?" Adar suggested. He must have known Elice was wavering. "That way, you can see my world and then go right back to hating me."

Too prideful to speak to him, she went to the door and stood with her back to him. She heard his soft steps as he came up behind her. Felt the heat of his body as he reached around her, his hand on the doorknob. He pulled it open and stepped out. She followed him down the stairs and past the guards. He held the outer door open for her and she crossed outside. The massive palace was still a shock to her senses. It seemed somehow more substantial and permanent than the ice walls of her own palace.

Something light draped across her head, hands brushing her shoulders. She shied away, glaring at Adar, at the silk cloth in his hands. "Elice, this headdress will keep you cool."

She drew upon winter, letting the cool settle around her. Gooseflesh rose on his arms. She stared at it, sudden understanding dawning. "If I can draw upon a trick of my magic in the heart of summer, then you could've used yours in winter."

Adar's hand fell to his side. "It's why I survived the sinking ship when none of my shipmates did. And all the times when I was sopping wet and my clothes were frozen to my body. I could even call up a little flame, though I didn't dare."

Feeling betrayed, Elice wrapped her arms around herself and glanced up at the sun hovering eerily in the middle of the sky. "Will it always be this way?" She wasn't sure if she was talking about the sun or her feeling of betrayal, or both.

He followed her gaze. "Here, the sun bisects the sky. The heat is worse during midday and better in winter. But it's always hot."

That Adar knew her well enough to guess her thoughts annoyed her. "I should have listened to my mother," she said.

Ignoring the comment, he skirted the west side of the palace without looking to see if Elice followed. She considered fleeing back inside the tower, but her feet moved after him, seemingly of their own accord.

When Adar turned into a smaller, simpler building, Elice hesitated at the darkened doorway. A distinctly animal smell came from inside the building. She stepped slowly forward. Everything was carved from rich, dark wood. Some kind of dried grass at her feet exuded a rich, loamy scent.

Before her was a long line of gates. One of them was open, and she could hear Adar's soft murmurs coming from inside. She stepped up beside it to find him putting some contraption into the mouth of a silver horse. The animal was much larger than Elice had expected—larger even than a polar bear. She froze for a moment, for she'd learned that the larger an animal, the more damage it could inflict.

"She won't hurt you." Adar tugged on a bit of leather trailing from the animal's mouth as she chewed lazily. He opened the gate, and Elice stepped back as the animal came through. She was beautiful and graceful and powerful. Elice was too overwhelmed to move.

Standing in the crook of the horse's neck, Adar had a hand around the animal's face, stroking the white markings. "Her name is Star. I trained her myself."

Elice found herself reaching toward the mare, who brought her nose closer and puffed moist breath against Elice's fingers. Then Star shook her head, put her muzzle to the flagstones, and blew. Adar placed a thick pad of wool and then a large leather contraption on the horse's back while she nibbled at the bits of dried grass she found on the flagstones.

Elice trailed her fingers across the horse's coarse mane. Then her fingers slid down Star's shoulder, which was silky with hard muscles underneath. She circled the animal, touching her, noting the way her hair lay. Star's flesh trembled when Elice lightly set a hand on her flank, but the horse didn't seem bothered by her presence.

Adar finished strapping on the contraption and stepped back. "Time to get on."

Elice turned to face him. "You want me to ride her?" The last time she'd tried to ride an animal hadn't worked out too well for her.

"I've wanted to show you the Summer Realm since the moment I met you. And we have a truce, remember?" He smiled.

She studied him and noticed the earnestness of his gaze. Her gaze strayed to his head. "What did you do to your hair?" she blurted.

He rubbed self-consciously at the thin bristling. "Burned it off."

Hesitantly, Elice reached out and ran the pads of her fingers along one of the tattooed patterns. Adar held very still and seemed to hold his breath. She stepped back, firmly reminding herself that she hated him. "I don't like it."

His mouth stretched as if he was fighting a smile. "The tattoos tell my life story. Sort of like—"

"Where's the line for liar?" she interrupted.

His shoulders stooped. "Sort of like your clannish belts."

"Is that another thing you stole from the clanlands?"

He rubbed his hand across his bald head. "We had a truce, remember?" When she didn't answer, he rested his head on the horse's muscular neck. "You don't understand, Elice. I'm trying to help you."

"Help me?" she shot back. "Kidnapping me is helping me?"

"You don't know what is at stake."

"Even if the Sundering is real, kidnapping me is going to stop it."

Adar looked up at her. "You don't know everything. And I cannot tell you all of it. But I have my reasons. If you believe nothing else, believe that."

She wanted to scream at him. Hit him again. But her body trembled instead. Because she believed him. Or was starting to, at least. "All right," she finally agreed. "I'll—I'll try."

A smile spread across Adar's face. "Good. Now, put your left foot in this stirrup, take hold of the horn, and pull yourself up into the saddle." He demonstrated, and she moved to obey.

Seconds later, Elice sat astride Star. The ground was much farther away than she preferred.

Adar led the mare out of the stable, and Elice saw a dozen guards astride their own horses—all of them brown with black manes and legs. The guards wore loose trousers, robes, and headscarves. One of the men was leading another horse, larger than the one Elice was on. Adar mounted another horse and led the way across the courtyard, the horses' hooves clacking against the flagstones. "A bailey," Elice said, suddenly remembering. "I read about those in my books."

Adar cocked an eyebrow at her. "The topics of your books seem oddly selective."

She shrugged. "My mother chose them, so yes."

The enormous gates were opened for them. Beyond were more, albeit smaller, palaces of stone. The city teemed with people, all of them wearing some form of trousers, with or without robes, and head coverings. They bowed when the troop passed. Her hand on her horse's neck, Elice studied the people—men and women, young and old, rich and poor. There were so many of them, with more appearing to replace any that left her sight. She felt dizzy from the sheer number. She'd never known how vast mankind was.

Elice noticed the wonderful aromas long before she saw the market, with roofs of colorful canvas providing shade for the thousands of wares. She was overwhelmed with the sights and smells and colors and sounds—so much more than she'd ever dreamed of.

"If it's too much, we can go back," Adar said after a while.

"No," Elice breathed. "I never want to go back."

At that, his face lit up. He started buying her things—plums, pears, figs, meat skewered on sticks and covered in sauces. If he saw her eyes lingering on a bolt of fabric or a pot, he bought it, and the guards placed it in a cart they hired, pulled by a man in sturdy robes.

When they passed an especially fine building, Elice noticed something glittering inside. "What's in there?"

Adar laughed. "You would notice the finest jewelry maker's shop in all of Idara." She blinked at him and frowned. He gestured to the cart. "Every item I've bought you, every single one, is the most expensive item to be found."

She smiled a little. "Can we go inside?"

He motioned to two of his guards, who went in before them and cleared out the building. Adar helped Elice dismount from the horse, and she let him, glad of their little truce. Being cruel to him was exhausting.

When they entered the building, her mouth came open. On every surface were clusters of jewels like bits of colored ice. Cases held dozens of glittering rings, necklaces, broaches, pendants, and bracelets in every imaginable color.

The shop's owner, a small man with stooped shoulders, bowed. "Prince Adar, I am most pleased to see you." His gaze moved to Elice. "Come to the back room, my dear. For it is there you will find my most valuable treasures."

He unlocked a door, and Elice followed him inside the small room. Here, the jewels were larger and more lustrous. She found herself handling the loose stones the most, as the shopkeeper put names to each and rattled off the details of their color and quality. Elice was entranced, until she came to the diamonds and opals—the same stones that her mother had set in her headdress.

She lifted a large opal and watched the colors trapped inside. Next, she picked up a diamond and watched the fire dance and flare within. Just like the prisms she made. Suddenly, Elice was struck with a homesickness so strong she thought it might kill her. She settled both stones back onto their velvet and turned her face to Adar.

"What did you do with the turquoise necklace?"

"I gave it to Sakari."

Elice nodded, glad her friend had it. "I think our truce is over."

"The lady does not wish to buy anything?" the shopkeeper asked, clearly disappointed.

Adar shook his head at the man, then led Elice back into the pounding sunlight. At that moment she realized her face and hands hurt and she was feeling ill.

A rush of movement made her turn to see a man dart around the guards. His eyes were calm and determined as he lifted a knife, arching it toward her. Adar hauled Elice back and stepped in front of her. His sword shot up, catching the man's blade even as the man's hand caught fire, blackening as Elice watched.

Before she could draw breath to scream, it was over. The guards took hold of the man's arms and forced him to his knees. He spit at Elice. "The Winter Queen deserves to know how it feels to lose a child! Deserves to know what it feels like to have a piece of her soul torn away. To feel bloody and raw—" The man broke off into sobs.

Elice stared at him in horrified fascination. The guards looked questioningly at Adar, who nodded. He took hold of Elice's shoulders and steered her toward the horses. Different guards converged around them, swords drawn.

She started to look back, but Adar held her more firmly. "Don't."

"Why?" Then she heard the singing of the sword. The man's insults ended with a wet thump. "You killed him!" Elice gasped.

Adar helped her onto the mare. "Uncontestable murder, attempted murder, or rape is treated with immediate beheading in Idara."

She couldn't stop herself from glancing back and immediately wished she hadn't. The blood and the neck stump would forever be burned in her memory. "What if he had escaped?"

Adar nudged his horse forward. "He would have been hunted down by the bounty hunters. They would only need to bring back his head to collect their money."

Elice looked out over the crowd, noticing darkness and danger where before she'd only seen wonder and motion. "My mother warned me about the darkness of men."

"I can't deny it, Elly. But neither should you deny the light."

"I'd like to go back to the palace now."

They rode back in silence. Elice no longer watched the people or studied their wares. Adar prattled on about his other home in the Adrack, the rust-red cliffs and narrow canyons filled with turquoise water.

"What does it matter?" she finally asked. "I'll never see it."

He fell silent after that. Soon, the enormous gates of the palace swung open and the horses' hooves rang off the flagstones. They reached the barn, where Adar helped Elice dismount. As her legs took her full weight, she groaned at the tenderness in her thighs and backside. After a moment, the stiffness faded and she walked awkwardly back into the sunshine. Once more she flinched at the strength of it. She didn't have to be told to head back to her tower; in fact she was eager for it.

Adar walked beside her. "Why are you doing this?" she finally asked. "Why feign kindness anymore? You already have what you want."

"Do I?" he said bitterly.

Elice glanced at him, wondering if he'd accidentally grown fond of her in their travels across the frozen wasteland of the Winter Queendom. "You didn't answer my question."

"I want you to experience the Summer Realm. I want you to have at least some good memories of this place—of me."

She looked over his shoulder, at the gates she'd crossed through twice. With a start, she realized this was where her Uncle Bratton had died, before these very gates. This was where the first battle of the War of the Queens had begun. "My uncle died here."

Adar turned to see what she was staring at. "A lot of people died here. The ground was soaked with blood."

Elice studied the flagstones, imagining blood running beneath her feet. "Our nations, our families, our magic—all of it is at war."

"In that, we have everything in common," Adar said softly.

Silently they walked back into the cool shadows of the tower and up the steps. They opened the doors to Elice's prison to find Cinder sitting at the table, stitching another overdress, this one turquoise.

As the other woman looked at Elice, her half smile faded. She pushed herself up from the table. "I told you to cover her head with a scarf!"

Adar seemed taken back. "She can pull enough winter to keep herself cool, Cinder."

"It wasn't the heat I was worried about." Cinder shot a glare at him and gestured for Elice to follow her into the bedroom. "We don't have your dark skin, Idaran. Get me some aloe. Now."

Adar started after them. "Why? What's wr—"

"She's burned, you idiot. Did you not notice how red her skin is?"

"I thought that's what happened to all clanmen in the heat."

In response, Cinder slammed the bedroom door in his face.

Elice touched her cheeks, noting the heat lingering in her skin. She flooded it with cold and immediately felt relief. "What's wrong?"

"The sun has burned your skin," Cinder said as she dipped some scraps of linen in a bowl of water. She dabbed Elice's forehead. "It's going to hurt today and worse tomorrow. And in about a week, you'll peel."

Elice touched her rough lips, feeling the tender throb. "I didn't know the sun could burn me."

"Everything in Idara burns," Cinder said bitterly.

A dar leaned over the table, gesturing with his arms. "How many times do I have to apologize? I didn't know," he said softly so as not to wake Elice, who still slept in the next room.

"Well," Cinder huffed. She stabbed her needle in and out of the fabric. "You can't take her out today. Her skin will burn even more easily than it did yesterday."

He sat back in exasperation. "But Cinder, she deserves to know the truth."

"You could just tell her."

Adar hesitated. "She'd never believe me."

"And you think my grandmother will make a difference?"

He stared at the closed door, wondering how much longer Elice would sleep. "I've taken so much from her, I'd like to give her this."

Cinder pushed out of her chair and rested her hands on the table. "What exactly do you expect my grandmother to give her?"

Adar and Cinder glared at each. "Maybe nothing, maybe something."

She pointed a large needle at his head. "Not today. Tomorrow, perhaps."

"There might not be a tomorrow." Not if Elice was executed tomorrow. And if she wasn't, Adar would be. He rubbed at his temples. He'd been up all night trying to figure out how to make her fall in love with him while also convincing her that the Sundering was real. This was the best he could come up with. "It's today or not at all."

"She's been through enough." Cinder swung her needle like a sword.

The door pushed open. Elice stood there in nothing but her underdress. Which might have sent a half dozen unchaste thoughts through Adar's head if her face weren't painfully red and covered in a green slime—another item he could tack to the list under "my fault."

"I'll go," Elice said.

Cinder set the needle on the tabletop and sighed. "The Adrack is no place for a woman already sun-sick."

Elice's gaze locked on Adar's, and he felt a flash of heat from her gaze. "I'll be ready in a minute," she said.

Elice shut the door and hurried to the bathroom. Looking in the mirror, she winced at the sight of the dried green goop on her face. She wet a towel and began gently rinsing it off to reveal her tender, shockingly red skin.

Cinder pushed into the bathroom behind her. "You should stay here and rest."

Elice squinted through the water running in her eyes. "Is sunburn really that dangerous?" Cinder hesitated, confirming what Elice suspected. The other woman had another reason for not wanting her to go. "Just say it."

Cinder let out a long breath and rested her shoulder against the doorframe. "I know Adar fairly well—I've known him since I was a girl. I can't think of a reason for him to take you there, but he always has a reason for everything he does. His refusing to tell me the reason makes me nervous. Besides, I thought you two hated each other."

Figuring it would hurt too much, Elice didn't bother toweling off. "I still hate him, but we sort of have a truce when it's convenient for me."

Cinder rolled her eyes and went into the other room. Within seconds she returned, carrying the turquoise overdress. It had a dozen gathers at the waist, emphasizing Elice's soft curves. This time, she let Cinder drape a scarf around her head and tie it in place, then pin a veil over her face so only her eyes showed. "That will prevent you from burning any worse than you already have. But you must keep your skin cool."

Back outside the tower, Elice found a net with thousands of fairies holding it. She balked at the sight. "Where are we going?"

"To my father's people, in the canyons of the Adrack," Adar answered.

"Can't we ride Star?"

"Only camels cross the desert, and that would take weeks. This way, we'll be there in a couple of hours."

Elice braced herself and climbed inside her net as Adar got in his. The fairies took flight. Soon they left the metropolis of Thanjavar behind and crossed a flat, barren plain. If not for the tans and reds and occasional blacks, Elice might have mistaken it for the frozen wastes of the Winter Queendom.

Finally, she saw red cliffs rising above the surface of the desert. Deep fissures ran through the surface. In the wider ones, Elice caught sight of emerald green and flashes of turquoise. Finally, the cliffs receded, leaving a wide opening. The fairies gently lowered her beside a brilliant-turquoise pool surrounded by a ring of jade. Only when the net touched down and the fairies slipped away did Elice notice the caves honeycombing the cliffs.

It was so green here, a shocking contrast to the rusty cliffs. Her mind put together bits and pieces of everything she'd learned, and she realized she was looking at an orchard. "Trees." The word slipped out on a breath.

"Date and coconut, but those aren't doing very well," Adar said as he moved to stand beside her. Elice moved past him and came up to a tree with crisscrossed bark. She stooped to pick up a furry-looking rock.

"A coconut," Adar said. "It was in the soup you ate yesterday."

She wrinkled her nose. "I ate a rock?"

He laughed. "It's more like a really big nut."

"Can't your mother just force the fairies to make the plants grow?"

"You know the Balance better than that. For a jungle to thrive there must also be a desert." Adar bent down, dug out a chunk of packed soil, and held it in his hands. "My tribesmen have done well enough on our own for centuries. We've engineered irrigation systems through all the canyons and beyond, as far as the water will reach. But the water isn't our biggest problem." He tossed a chunk of dirt, which broke apart. "Sand and clay and silt do not make for hardy crops."

He strode on, brushing his hands off on his trousers. "Still, we tribesmen manage to grow date palms and mesquite pods, lima beans and buffalo gourds. We also grow moringa, baobab, acacias, and chaya leaves. Where the canyons are wider, we grow wheat and some other grains."

Above them, Elice noticed a blur of movement. At first she thought it was a fairy, but it was only a bird, though far different from the sea birds she was used to. This one seemed to mirror the landscape, bright blue with a rusty back. It was so beautiful. But then it made a horrible gawking sound at them.

Elice blinked in surprise. "I expected something . . . prettier to come from such a pretty bird."

"That kind will dive at you, too."

Elice decided maybe it wasn't so pretty after all. She explored the shady grove of palm trees, keeping a wide berth from any insects after her experience in the tundra. They found a lizard and a snake, which Adar told her to always avoid. They also found a scorpion, which looked terrifying, but he said they tasted pretty good—once their tails were cut off. Elice found the idea repulsive, but he had thought raw meat repulsive too, so she determined to keep an open mind.

"Why did you bring me here, Adar?" she asked finally. "It can't be to show me crops."

He nodded. "Follow me."

When they left the cover of the grove, the wind picked up, bringing with it a stench like rot and human waste. Elice covered her nose with her hand. They came upon a man using a shovel to open a divot. Adar and Elice watched as water sluiced through a channel built into the canyon walls.

Adar paused when the canyon unexpectedly opened up, revealing a little side canyon with a well-worn path leading down it. Deep inside was a huge mound of rotting scraps and feces. "After the harvest, everyone helps dung the trees."

Elice grimaced. "It's one thing to use dung as fuel for a fire. Another to spread it around plants, which you then eat."

Adar laughed. "Come on, there's more I want to show you."

As soon as they passed the canyon, the smell was gone. Breathing deeply in relief, Elice glanced back at the man still working the canals. He opened a second gate and water rushed out.

Passing more crops, she and Adar wove through the winding canyon, which began to narrow. Voices echoed off the walls. Lots of voices. They rounded a corner and her feet stopped of their own accord.

Below her was a round courtyard with a fountain in the middle. Surrounding it were a multitude of women scrubbing out their clothing in the basin, while children splashed around them. They were all darker skinned, with thick black hair, delicate features, and robes that varied in length from below the knees to the ground. Trees grew on raised beds, providing shade to more women who worked over smoking ovens, sweat running down their temples.

There was laughter and scolding and singing, a raucous noise that left Elice feeling lightheaded. She stood for a long time, marveling at them. She could have watched them forever. But then a child, a naked little boy, noticed her and Adar. He came running up the hill on short legs before launching himself at Adar. "Dar!" he squealed.

Adar picked the child up and patted his back. Elice stared. She'd seen a few children at the highmen village, but only from a distance. *Was I ever that small?*

Now, more of the women noticed Adar. They called out their greetings, leaving their washing and their looms to climb toward him. They were all sound and faces and movement, all of which seemed to be directed at her. Elice started to shrink back, but Adar gripped her hand.

She tried to send him a shock of cold, but he only smiled a little and held on tighter. "They're my family. My aunts and cousins."

The women descended on him, hugging and kissing and laughing. Elice watched, desperate to get away, yet somehow wanting to stay. Though they were speaking Idaran, the words battered her like an angry ocean—waves of sound breaking up and over her, leaving her gasping for breath. Adar made them promises, something about eating. Then he took Elice's arm, led her through the throng to the other side of the clearing, and started up a narrow canyon.

It was cool in the shadows; Elice got the feeling the sun never directly reached the canyon floor. And there was a breeze—hot, but refreshing nonetheless. Here women worked a hinged wooden contraption that crushed long stalks.

"Flax." Adar pointed at the stalks. "They're crushing out the brittle parts, leaving the flexible fibers."

A young girl took a bundle and ran it farther up the canyon, where she set it with dozens of other bundles. A woman took one of the bundles and scraped it between a board and a large, flat stick. Farther still up the canyon, women used what looked like a large wooden brush to comb out the flax.

"That makes the fibers line up."

More women took the fibers and wove them through a loom. Adar paused beside an older woman wearing a veil, her hands deftly working the shuttle. Elice watched her for a moment, entranced by her precision.

Adar touched her shoulder. "Storm, there's someone I'd like you to meet."

Jumping a little in surprise, the woman turned. Elice's gasp caught in her throat. She was obviously clannish. Though pure white, her hair must have once been blonde. Her features were proud and fine, though her skin was dotted with age spots and lined with wrinkles. But it was the eyes that gave her away—eyes the dark charcoal of a thundercloud.

Elice stepped forward and reached out to touch the woman's skin, who looked curiously at her but did not shy away from the touch. "My grandfather had a sister taken captive by the Idarans when she was a young woman," Elice said. "Her name was Storm." Elice had heard the story only once, and her grandfather had not been the same for months after the telling of it.

Storm's head came up. "Otec?" she whispered.

"Yes," Elice managed, her voice cracking. She pulled out her pendant and showed it to the other woman.

85

Storm's fingers grazed the raised edges. "He always loved carving—he'd make toys for the village children." Tears slipped down the old woman's cheeks, and she looked around in shock. "But what are you doing here?"

Elice clenched her teeth and her fists, a whole line of tension that locked her body up. "My mother is Ilyenna, daughter of Otec, and Queen of Winter. Adar lured me out of the Winter Queendom, where I was taken by the Summer Queen to serve as bait to trap my mother."

Storm shot Adar a look of churning anger. "You betrayed my great-niece?"

He sighed. "Would you believe me if I told you I had good reasons?"

"Then Cinder is my cousin," Elice gasped. "You are my great-aunt." She felt overwhelmed with the sense that she came from somewhere. That she belonged.

Storm stepped closer to Elice, her hands smoothing over her cheeks and lingering on her hazel eyes before she took a lock of Elice's dark hair in her hand. "But who gave you this coloring, child?"

Elice frowned. Of all the questions she thought Storm might ask, this wasn't one. "My grandmother was a highwoman. Her name was Matka."

"That cannot be." Storm dropped the lock of hair as if it had burned her.

"Otec and Matka are my mother's parents. My father is Rone, son of Seneth and Narium of the Argons."

Storm turned to Adar, and some silent communication passed between them. "This is why you insisted on Cinder?"

"Partly," Adar replied.

Storm motioned for Elice to follow her.

"What is it?" Elice asked warily.

Without answering, the old woman abandoned her loom and took Adar and Elice to a narrow opening in the wall. An incense lantern swung above them, smoke flowing out of it. "To keep the fairies away," Storm muttered.

Inside was a large cavern with beams of light refracting at a million sharp angles. Elice glanced far above and found small openings surrounded by mirrors. The beams of light landed on dozens of tents, colors bright where the light hit them, and then mute again where it fell away. Elice felt dizzy from the colors and the incense smoke curling from blocks before all the entrances.

Storm led them into a tent with walls made of woven landscapes of high mountains, capped in white and rimmed in emerald. Beneath Elice's feet, the rug resembled a field of grain, and pillows of dozens of different flowers lined the floor. There was even a village on the far panel, the houses made of round stones.

"It's like my room," Elice said in wonder.

"It's the clanlands, child. The home of my youth." Storm pulled out more squares of sticky, tarlike incense, placed them in shallow bowls all around the walls of the tent, and pressed the flame of her lamp to each until they began to smoke.

While she worked, Elice circled the square tent. The first panel featured the village surrounded by green. In the next, the mountains were bedecked in crimson and gold, with amber fields on the rolling hills. The next panel showed mounds of snow weighing down the pine trees like a too-heavy coat. The final panel was a riot of color—blooms of lilac and mountain daisy and a dozen other flowers.

Elice circled back to the first panel and stepped closer to the flock of sheep. A boy was there, a dog at his feet. The barefoot boy held a shepherd's crook in his hand. "I have nearly the same image in the walls of my home," Elice whispered.

"That's where I first recognized them," Adar replied. "I thought you must have spent some of your childhood in the clanlands."

Storm was suddenly beside her. "That's your grandfather, Otec."

Elice ran a finger along his outline and let her fingers rest on the dog. Suddenly she remembered. "His name was Freckles."

She turned to Storm and saw tears fill the old woman's eyes again. "I never knew what happened to my brother," Storm said quietly. "He was the only one of us not taken."

"He had two children, Ilyenna and Bratton," Elice told her. "Bratton became High Chief of all the clans—he led the clanlands as they invaded Idara. It was there that Nelay killed him."

Storm's breath caught, and she turned an angry glare to Adar. "Get out."

He pressed his lips into a hard line. "I need to hear this just as much as she does. I'm staying." The way he said it with such finality, Elice knew he meant it.

Storm seemed to know it too. Easing down onto some cushions on the floor, she motioned for Elice to join her. "Tell me more."

Elice knelt before the older woman. "Bratton married Larina Bend—"

Storm snorted. "A Bend? I'm sure he had his hands full. Old money there, and not the good kind."

Elice didn't know how to respond, so she continued on. "Together, they had eight children—all of them boys. Five of them died in the war, the rest made it home. The oldest living son is now the clan chief."

Storm's gaze was distant. "And is the clan house filled with the voices of children again?"

"My grandfather said it was."

Storm finally met Elice's gaze. "Why did he leave?"

Elice smiled a little. "Grandfather always said his grandsons didn't need him anymore, but his granddaughter did."

Storm hesitated before reaching out and taking Elice's hand in her own. She rubbed her thumb across Elice's knuckles. "Tell me more about your grandmother."

"She was an artist, like you and me, and she loved drawing with charcoal. Grandfather used to buy her vellum whenever he could. She drew landscapes, mostly of the clanlands, but sometimes other places. Grandfather keeps them in a chest in his room with some of his carvings. He showed them to me every once in a while."

Storm seemed instantly angry. "Did any of these landscapes ever look like Idara?"

At the look in the old woman's eyes, Elice felt a strong foreboding that Storm held some secret Elice didn't want to know. "Yes," Elice said in a whisper.

Storm looked at the meadow beneath her feet. "Your grandfather married a traitor—an Idaran."

Elice wanted to laugh, but the look of hurt in the old woman's eyes couldn't be denied. "My grandmother was a highwoman," she said carefully.

Storm grunted. "Half. They were all half Idaran and half highman. The Raiders came pretending to be ambassadors from the Highlands, but they were really infiltrators. They attacked the Shyle and killed any who resisted, as well as any men who hadn't already left to fight the Idarans gathering along the coast. They planned to attack the clanlands from two fronts, leaving us with only enough Idarans to guard us."

Storm stared at the image of the Shyle village, her face hard and bitter. "I don't know what happened. Otec had taken Matka into the mountains, but then she was back with us and they wanted her dead. They thought we would kill her; she was one of their priestesses and they feared to harm her themselves." Storm gave a bitter chuckle. "I would have killed her—started to—but Holla begged me to stop. And no one could deny Holla anything. Not even me."

Elice had heard stories of Holla, a woman with the mind of a child. Her grandfather had always spoken her name with reverence and longing, as if he missed her more than the others.

"Then something went wrong," Storm went on. "The Idarans took us and fled. I only saw Otec two more times, both when he was fighting to free us." Her eyes slipped closed as if the memories were too much. "In the end, he had a choice—to save us or save the clanlands. I told him to go, but inside, I wanted him to stay. To save us. I hated myself, hated him, for choosing them over me. Sometimes I still do."

Elice suddenly realized Cinder had said her grandmother and mother had been sold into a brothel. No wonder Storm resented Otec. If she'd known what was before them, would she have chosen differently?

Storm looked up, her eyes dry, her face brittle as old bones. "Every day I try to forgive him, forgive myself. Some burdens you can never put down but must simply struggle to carry. But I would see him again. I would see my homeland and my people."

"Nelay doesn't know who you are?" Elice whispered.

"Idara leaves me alone, and I leave them alone," Storm scoffed.

Elice glanced at Adar. "But you said this part of the canyons was for your family. If so, why is Storm here?"

"Storm's daughter, Ash, married one of my cousins, Ashar," Adar said.

"Yes," Storm said softly. "And Cinder married another cousin, Darsam. Both are good men."

Elice looked between them. "Ash is Cinder's mother?"

Storm nodded softly. "I named her to remind my offspring that we can rise from the embers and ashes."

"How did she get free?" Elice asked.

Storm sighed and lay back against the cushions. "That's a story for another time, and it is Cinder's story to tell. Leave me now. The old memories are stirred up, and I must beat them down."

Elice wanted to stay, wanted to learn more, but Adar reached out and touched her hand. "We need to head back before it's too dark." She rose to her feet and turned to go.

"Wait," Storm called. She went to a carved trunk beneath the tapestry of the village and pulled something out. She cradled it in her hands and then looked up at Elice, tears streaming down the lines in her face. Without a word, she held it out for Elice to take. Elice opened her palm and looked at the small carving inside. It was one half of a beaver that had been cut perfectly in half.

"It was Holla's. Tell Otec I took care of her. She raised my daughter while I worked in the brothel. And she was happy."

Elice stared at the beaver, the edges worn smooth and shiny from years of handling. She'd seen its mate—the exact replica—inside her grandfather's chest. "And his brothers and other sisters?"

"I searched for years but never found them." Storm wiped the tears from her eyes.

Elice stepped forward and pressed a kiss to the old woman's cheek. "He never stopped missing you. I'm not sure he ever forgave himself, either."

Storm closed Elice's hands around the carving. "You give him this, and you tell him about me. Tell him my child and grandchild are happy."

But there was something else in Storm's hand too—a dagger about the length of her palm, with a wicked point. "A clanwoman always carries a knife," she said softly. "And knows how to use it."

Elice swallowed hard as she tucked the knife beneath her belt, inside a little pocket her mother had sewn into the leather. "Thank you." Storm curled up with one of her flower pillows and stared at her village, a look of longing on her face.

When Adar and Elice reached the outside and she could feel the sun on her face again, she took a deep breath and asked, "Why did Storm stay here? Why didn't she go back to the Shyle?"

"The same reason your grandfather didn't go back," Adar said. "You needed him in the Winter Queendom. Storm's daughter and granddaughter need her here."

Elice closed her eyes, realizing just how much her grandfather had given up to raise her. "Why did you bring me to this place?"

"Because I wanted you to know who you are, and I knew you wouldn't take my word for it."

"When did you figure it out—who my grandmother is?"

"Matka is an Idaran name. It means 'mother,'" Adar answered. Elice gave a bitter chuckle, but he continued, "Your mother is a quarter Idaran, and you're an eighth. You can't hate something that's a part of yourself."

Elice whirled on him. "Storm and her daughter were both forced into a brothel because of Idarans."

"And your grandmother was raised an Idaran," Adar said carefully.

Elice faltered. "Half!" she spat. "She left them, didn't she? She became a clanwoman." She spun around, refusing to look at him anymore. "What exactly are you trying to prove?"

He touched her arm, but she shrugged him off. "I'm half Idaran, Elice. I've spent half my life in Idara and half in the Adrack, as have my brothers and sisters. There are some . . . dark things about Idara. But there is also so much good. And much has changed since Queen Parisa took over. There are no more slaves. Idara doesn't raid anymore. Can you look at our goodness and let go of our bad? Can you forgive us, please?"

"You think that by making me less hateful toward Idara you will somehow get me to forgive you?" Elice stalked away. "Take me home, Adar. Our truce is over for the day."

"There is one more thing for you to see. Then you can go home."

Seething, she turned to find him heading deeper into the cave. She considered not following him, yet she knew him well enough to realize he wouldn't take her back until he'd shown her what he wanted her to see. She stormed after him. They climbed to another level and then Adar started up a wood-and-sinew ladder. Elice followed, not feeling entirely safe.

After what seemed like forever, they emerged onto a flat plateau of rusty rocks. Adar strode across the surface. "There are other canyons in the Adrack filled with groves and crops and people. Dozens of them." He paused at the edge of a cliff and looked down. Elice hesitated before stepping up beside him and looking down.

There was nothing there. Not nothing like an empty canyon, but nothing like a gash in the world that bled darkness. Elice's mouth came open. "What is down there?"

He scooped up a fist-sized rock and hurled it over the edge. She watched it until she couldn't see it anymore. "Nothing. A crevasse this deep should be filled with water. But as far as we can tell, it never ends."

Elice looked to the left and right, noting how the rift narrowed at the ends. "Are there more?"

"Not yet." Adar brushed his hands off. "Do you believe in the Sundering now?"

She opened her mouth, closed it again. But how could she deny it after everything she'd seen. "I'm not sure I'm strong enough to say it out loud."

He took a step closer to her. "Elice . . ."

She shut her eyes. "How can I not believe after everything I have seen?" The guilt nearly overwhelmed her. "What do I have to do with any of this?"

He turned to her and she saw the fear in his eyes, and a hurt so deep it made her breath catch. "Adar? What is it?"

"Remember when I asked you what you would give up to save the world?" Warily, she nodded, and he said, "What if you could save just one person, but it would cost you everything? What would you give up then?"

Elice sensed he was talking about something important. "I guess that would depend on the person."

"If it was someone I loved, I would give up everything—even my own life." Adar turned and walked away without looking back.

Desperate to escape thoughts of the Sundering, Elice studied Cinder, trying to find something of herself in the other woman. After all, they both had Clannish and Idaran blood. But they were almost exact opposites. Cinder had golden skin, blonde hair, and gray eyes. Elice had pale skin, black hair, and dark-hazel eyes. But there was something in the way they were built—bodies lithe and yet soft.

"Did you know that my grandfather and your grandmother are brother and sister?" Elice asked.

Cinder's head darted up from her work. "What?"

"Otec is my grandfather." She told Cinder the rest.

That night, they lay in the same bed, telling stories of their childhoods. Cinder's hadn't been a pleasant one, but she'd managed to free herself and her mother and grandmother from the brothel. She'd even convinced a young prince—Adar—to change the laws so that slavery was abolished in Idara.

"I think I could forgive him for kidnapping me from the queendom," Elice confided. "He was just trying to end the war. But I can't forgive him for tricking me into falling in love with him so I would go with him. Especially when he knew he would betray me in the end."

"That doesn't sound like Adar," Cinder said as she rolled over to face the ceiling.

"What do you mean? He is a big flirt."

Cinder chuckled. "More like a tease than a flirt. You should see him with his sisters."

Elice rolled her eyes. "You can't tell me he's not a rake."

"Yes, the girls love him, but he never knows what to do with them after he's caught them. So he just moves on to the next one. You're the first girl I've ever seen stick."

Elice snorted. "He tried to leave me behind too. More than once."

"Because he cares about you and didn't want you caught up in all this. There's no other reason for him to have stuck around this long."

Elice mulled over the idea. "But he still betrayed me."

They were silent for a time before Cinder said, "Do you love him?"

"Of course not!" Elice knew her words sounded a little too sharp and a little too vehement.

Cinder let out a girlish giggle. "I think you must forgive him," she said in mockingly formal tones.

Elice rolled over. She didn't want to talk to Cinder anymore. It only seemed a moment later that Elice woke to the sound of the door opening and saw Adar standing there. "I wondered where you were," he said to Cinder.

She squinted at him and then looked out the window at the dim morning beyond. "Why are you here so early?"

He gave a smile that seemed forced. "Lots to do today. Elice, get ready. I have another friend I want you to meet."

She groaned. "Not another one. I don't need any more revelations."

Adar rested his hip on the doorframe, then folded his arms and studied her. "Are you sure?" he asked seriously. "I, for one, would rather know the truth."

So he did have more revelations. Why was he pushing all this on Elice?

Cinder sat up and chucked her pillow at him before collapsing back on the bed. He caught it with a grin. "Come on! I brought fig cakes for breakfast."

Cinder shot up, hair sticking up all over. "I get the bathroom first!" She disappeared from sight.

Elice rolled her eyes and turned over with every intention of going back to sleep. But then a delicious, sweet smell set her mouth to watering and there was no going back. Still half asleep, she stumbled out of bed and followed the aroma.

Adar was seated next to the fig cakes, which looked like a fluffy bread covered in something shiny and brown. He broke one off and offered it to Elice. She held it in her hand and sniffed it, then took a bite. Sweetness exploded across her tongue, along with pieces of pasty figs and crunchy pecans. Adar watched her eat with an unnerving expression. She'd eaten a dozen fig cakes by the time Cinder showed up,

The other woman stopped dead. "You've eaten most of them!" Feeling guilty, Elice paused in the middle of devouring another. Cinder grabbed the remaining cakes and huffed over to the other side of the table.

"Sorry," Elice mumbled around her mouthful.

"Elice chose fig cakes over primping," Adar said with laughter in his voice. "You can't blame her for being smarter than you."

Cinder shot them both a glare, her mouth too full of fig cakes for a rebuttal. Elice licked syrup off her lips. Adar chuckled and Elice turned to find him staring at her mouth. Disconcerted, she scooted a little farther over in her chair.

He bit his lip, obviously trying to keep from smiling. "You have a little honey on your chin."

Elice licked her fingers and rubbed at her chin. "Did I get it?"

He covered his mouth with his hand. "There's some on your cheek too."

She licked her other fingers and rubbed her cheek. "How about now?"

There was no denying the laughter in his eyes. "There's some on your forehead too."

Elice rolled her eyes. "This is why I wait to bathe until after I eat."

She left the room, not feeling nearly as angry as she had pretended to be. Wanting to look really nice, she took a little more time with her hair than was necessary. Morosely, she stared at her red, flaking skin. But there was no help for it. With the realization that she wanted to look nice for Adar, Elice thrice cursed herself.

When she came out, Cinder was gone and a man had taken her place, his back to Elice as he pored over a book. The air practically choked with incense—this must be a meeting they didn't want any fairies overhearing. Elice tried not to feel abandoned; after all Cinder wasn't really her friend, even if she was family. More like her minder and seamstress all in one.

Coughing, Elice waved the smoke away. The man turned around and she gasped. He could have been Adar's twin. They were both tall with the same high forehead, strong nose, and nearly black eyes. Adar had been telling her the truth about the blossom keeping his father young.

He smiled gently when he saw Elice. He rose to meet her and squeezed her hand with fingers that were calloused and stained with ink. "I'm Rycus, Denar's father." His voice was low and rumbling.

She looked between the two. "Denar?" Had Adar lied about his name?

"My full name is Adar Denar Rycus ShaBejan," Adar said. "It's customary for the tribesmen to call their firstborn sons after their mother's father out of respect."

"Why are you here?" she directed the question at Rycus.

"Right to the point," Rycus said with a wink to Adar. "I like her." He gestured with large hands to the books covering the table. "Has Denar—Adar," he corrected himself, "managed to convince you that the Sundering is real? That the past ages were real?"

Elice lifted her gaze in silent agony. If she admitted the Sundering was real, she was admitting her mother's wrath had caused it. And Elice had sealed her mother's wrath the day her father died.

Perhaps misinterpreting her lack of response, Rycus said, "Imagine that every age does end with the death of the old magic and the birth of the new. When the new age begins, many things of the old age are gone forever, and many new things have taken the place of the old ones."

"Any records of such creatures would probably be destroyed by the Sundering," Adar added. "So all that would have survived are stories, told from one person to the next. Those stories would be jumbled and the details lost over time, but they would exist because that old world existed."

Rycus nodded, his eyes sparkling. "There are truths hidden in the old fables. Truths and histories."

Elice finally spoke. "I still don't understand what any of this has to do with me."

Adar sat back in his chair. "Two fairies came to us a couple of years ago."

"So?" Elice shrugged.

The two men exchanged glances. "One of those fairies was Chriel," Rycus said.

Elice gasped. "Chriel? But . . . that's impossible. She's a winter fairy. She wouldn't have survived here."

"She and another fairy, Nagale, were the ones who told us about you," Rycus explained.

"Though she left out certain details and flat-out lied about others," Adar muttered before straightening up and clearing his throat. "Nagale led my ship to the Winter Palace. Chriel guaranteed us safe passage."

Between ragged breaths, Elice asked, "Chriel told you to lure me away?" It wasn't possible. It couldn't be.

"She claimed to be one of the very first fairies," Rycus answered. "She said she remembers the last unicorn. She saw dwarves and elves mix with mankind. And as the unicorn's magic faded away, more fairies came into existence."

"But why would she betray me?" Elice choked out. "And then defy the queen to her death?"

Pain flashed across Adar's face. "I didn't know she meant to do that. But I think, perhaps, she was trying to force you to leave the queendom."

"Why me?" Elice held out her empty palms.

Rycus sighed. "The original plan was to force a peaceful surrender in exchange for your safe return."

She chewed the inside of her cheek. "Original plan?" Rycus shot Adar a glance, and something passed between them that Elice didn't understand. Dread shifted through her ribs and settled in her lower belly. "Tell me."

Adar looked down. "Elice, she isn't coming."

Elice shut her eyes and covered her mouth with her hand. Her throat worked as she tried to swallow the bile rising in her throat. One simple refusal had confirmed what she'd suspected for years: her mother didn't love her. Not in the ways a mother should.

Rycus leaned forward and said kindly, "Child, you need to understand something about becoming a fairy queen. It either burns or shatters the human soul. They are never quite . . . human anymore. They're a force of nature. You know this. Deep down, you have to know this."

Elice closed her eyes, remembering the cold, distant woman who left her alone for months at a time with nothing but the darkness and her grandfather for company. "Yes," Elice said softly and lifted her head. "But she is not evil."

"No," Rycus agreed. "But she isn't good, either."

Elice clasped her shaking hands. "She loves me and my father and my grandfather. Isn't that *good*? And besides, if my mother is broken, so is Nelay."

Adar looked to his father as if for help. Rycus quietly closed the old book. "Elice, was your mother not more human before your father died?"

"Yes."

"A consort has a softening effect on his queen," Rycus said. "Without your father, Ilyenna is more fairy than human."

"Why are you telling me this?"

"Because we think there might be another way," Rycus said.

Elice glanced up, hope mixing with the dread inside her in a sickening swirl.

Adar and Rycus shared a knowing look. "Maybe you should tell her," Adar finally said. "I have a feeling she'll be more likely to believe it coming from you."

Rycus eyed her, his expression unreadable. "You met one of my daughters, Zahra?" Elice nodded. "And did you notice her power over summer, like Adar's?"

Elice wet her lips. "No."

"That's because she doesn't have power over summer," Rycus answered. "None of my children do—except Adar."

"What does that have to do with anything?" she asked.

Rycus leaned forward. "You have powers too, Elice, just as he does. Have you never wondered why?"

"I didn't know he had powers at all until we came here. And since then, I've been pretty busy hating him."

Rycus watched her. "You are your mother's heir because she was pregnant with you when she became queen, as Nelay was pregnant with Adar."

Elice rubbed at the ache in her forehead with the heel of her palm. "That's impossible. My mother became the queen forty years ago. I am only seventeen."

"And how old is your grandfather?" Rycus asked.

She grew tired of this. "He is sixty."

"Yet his older sister, Storm, is in her eighties," Adar said.

Elice frowned. "Yes, his *older* sister."

"But only by a few years," Rycus said. "Otec is eighty-five. Both of your parents are in their sixties. And you, Elice, are forty years old."

She laughed at the ridiculousness of it. "Do I look forty to you?" Adar and Rycus only watched her, compassion in their gazes. She sighed. "I know the queens don't age, but I remember my father before he died. He was still a very young man. Had he lived, he would be the age you claim me to be."

"The Elice blossom," Rycus said softly. "Nelay gives it to Jezzel and me every year. We're both over forty and still look like youths."

Elice turned away from them. "The Summer Queen has the blossom, not my mother."

"Not at first," Rycus said. "Leto—the previous Summer Queen—must have given the blossom to your mother, who in turn gave it to your grandfather, your father, and you."

Elice pushed to her feet and began pacing. "I would have twenty more years of memories!" She wished Adar would stop looking at her.

"Not if you were a very young child," he said.

She froze in her tracks. "You're saying I was an infant for twenty years? But why? Why would they keep me as a baby?"

Adar shook his head. "Not an infant. A toddler."

Elice felt dizzy and hollow. She braced herself against the back of the chair. "I can't—I don't believe you."

Adar reached a hand toward her, but she pulled away. "Think of the trees of your room, Elice. You knew the proportions of the pine needles, the creased shape of a blade of grass, even the soft spines of a poppy."

"The pictures in the books—" she began.

"Are a poor replica for real life," Adar said. "Only someone who'd experienced summer could have known those details."

Elice was dizzy and her hands felt numb.

"Think of the landscapes you carved into the ice," Adar continued. "The same landscapes Storm wove into the walls of her tents."

"My grandfather described them for me so many times . . ." Elice's words trailed off uncertainly.

She looked up at Adar, her gaze begging him to tell her this wasn't true. He pressed his lips in a thin line and forged on. "Have you ever tasted an elice blossom?"

The memory came swift and sudden. It was one of the first days of spring, when Elice's mother had returned from spreading winter. The sun was back, vanishing the never-ending dark. And Elice's father was so happy. The Winter's End ceremony should start any moment, but they were putting it off. Playing first.

Her father chased Elice through the palace, dancing and laughing through the throne room. Her mother caught up to them, her aurora wings surrounding them with colors that Elice had never stopped craving. Wrapped up in her father's arms, with sunlight drifting through the columns, Elice felt the hole inside her fill up.

Her mother stood before Elice. "Here, my girl, I brought you something."

"A present?" Elice squealed.

Her mother held out a single petal, white with a burgundy center and a yellow tip. Elice rubbed the petal in her hand, relishing the impossible softness.

"Ilyenna . . ." Rone said. "You promised."

"Just let me keep her little a while longer. I will only ever have one child, Rone."

Elice looked between her mother and father, not understanding the tension between them. Her mother smiled one of her rare smiles. The smile that softened her hard face into something almost gentle. "Put it on your tongue, and the dream will come."

Elice did so eagerly, for the blossom always took her to a field of green so bright it hurt her eyes. There were new buds forming on the trees. The sun was directly above her instead of circling the horizon. There were mountains in the distance—mountains that seemed to cup the picturesque valley in the palms of their hands. Elice never wanted to leave this place, never wanted to go back to the endless cold.

Now, Elice raised haunted eyes to meet Adar's gaze. "They taste like summer." Somehow, the petals had taken her to the Shyle, which was how she knew what it was like. Why the mountains and trees of the Shyle adorned the walls of her room.

Adar nodded as if he could see the realization come over her. "I had an elice blossom a couple times," he said. "First when I took a crossbow quarrel to the back. Another time when it saved my life after the chariot accident, and I was never quite the same after."

Elice remembered the story about the chariot—how he'd wanted to teach some boys that had insulted his deformed sister. And she suddenly realized the sister he'd stood up for was Zahra. "Why are you telling me this?"

"Because you are your mother's heir." Adar came around the table, his arms reaching for Elice. She backed away. "Because you are the only one who can stop her."

Elice came up against the opposite wall, cool against the sweat gathered in the small of her back. "Stop her? I can't stop her."

"You alone can get close enough," Adar said. "As the new queen, you could declare peace and restore the Balance. Then the combined strength of summer and winter can stop the Sundering and redirect the magic into its new form."

Elice's mouth came open. "You want me to kill my mother." Their silence confirmed it. "I would never!"

"You're the only one who can get close enough," Rycus said, repeating his son's words.

Adar watched her, pity in his gaze. "Not even to save the world?"

Elice desperately shook her head. "You can't ask this of me." He started toward her, but she held out a staying hand. "I can't! I won't!" She was sobbing hard now, barely able to breathe.

Adar gathered her in his arms. Furious, she tried to resist, but he only held on tighter. "Don't, don't push me away. Please, Elice. We only have today."

She wavered. He had betrayed her, but he'd done it to save the world. He hadn't thought she would be harmed in the process. She crumbled, the sobs coming hard and fast. Adar's arms tightened around her as if he could keep her from breaking apart. When she finally managed to calm herself, Rycus was gone.

"I can't, Adar," Elice said between the shudders that follow a hard cry.

He stroked her hair. "Not even to save your grandfather? Your kin in the clanlands?"

She pulled back to look at him. "My grandfather?"

Adar opened his mouth, closed it again. "The Sundering could destroy us all."

Elice watched him with a furrowed brow. It seemed he'd started to say something else and then changed his mind. But perhaps she was reading too much into it. "You don't know that for certain," she said after a pause.

He let out a long sigh. "I have a gift for you." Adar held out the flower she had made for him.

"But I made that for you."

"I wanted to give you something equally as powerful—something I hoped you wouldn't throw away." A blue flame appeared in the center of the flower, casting cool light over the room. "Like your gift to me, the flame will never go out." Adar reached out and removed the chain that held her grandfather's little carving. Then he strung this new flower through it and settled it back around Elice's neck. "And you will never be in darkness again."

Tears sprang to her eyes. "What happens now?" she whispered.

"Tomorrow, you will meet with my mother before the gathered assembly."

"And then?"

She felt Adar's muscles tense. "I've sworn by the Balance not to tell you, but Elice"—he pulled back and looked into her eyes—"do you trust me?"

She looked from one of his eyes to the other, trying to read the sincerity of his gaze. His betrayal still stung, but she couldn't deny that he had done everything he could to protect her. "I want to."

"Then trust me when I say that I would give up my life before I would let any harm come to you."

10

Elice stood on the balcony, looking out at the city drenched in the gold of the rising sun. In her hand she clutched the pendants hanging from her neck. Thanjavar was beautiful, she realized. The people were not full of darkness, but neither were they full of light. They had a mix of both, and the one they nurtured was the one that shone through.

She heard steps behind her and turned to find Cinder with a white dress gathered in her arms. The interlocking patterns of the clans were stitched in gold on the hem. "You know how much I hate white!" Elice joked, trying to lighten the mood like Adar would have, but the words tasted like dust in her mouth.

"You are a princess of winter," Cinder replied. "You should look it."

"What fabric?"

"Silk." She helped Elice slip the dress over her head. It fluttered around her ankles like a spider web and felt as light as sunrays. She paused before the nightstand to take the half-beaver carving and tuck it firmly into her pocket. When she finished tying her gold-embroidered belt, Cinder had returned with a chest. She set it on a table and opened it. Inside were glittering jewels set in gold.

Elice pulled out a headdress of gold woven in the interlocking knots of the clanlands. There was a large, oval opal for her forehead. Elice fingered the headdress, realizing how much it resembled the one she'd left in the Winter Queendom, though this one was even more delicate.

"How did you know?" Elice asked.

Cinder shrugged. "I didn't."

Then Elice recognized the opal. She'd seen it in the jeweler's shop the day Adar had taken her to the market. She lifted the headdress and settled it onto her head. Cinder left Elice's hair long and wavy, with gold and jewels dangling from it. Once Cinder finished, Elice wandered over to a mirror. She certainly looked like a princess.

A knock sounded at the door in the other room. "It's time to go, Princess," called a voice she didn't recognize.

Elice started and backed away, then rushed into the bathroom and vomited the light supper she'd eaten earlier. When she'd spit the last of the bitter bile into the bowl, she rested her head on the cool marble tiles.

Cinder stood at the door. "Elice?"

She closed her eyes. "There are more days in a month than people I have actually spoken to. Now Nelay wants to present me before some crowd. She will use me as bait to trap my mother. And I don't know if she will hurt me." Perhaps more painful than all of that was Adar's betrayal. So painful that Elice couldn't even find the words to say it.

Cinder's feet made padding sounds as she entered the room. She knelt next to Elice and gently placed her hand on Elice's side. "When my grandmother was seventeen, she was taken as a slave by the Idarans and sold into a brothel. It should have broken her—she was meant to be broken. But she never forgot who she was, and she didn't let me forget, either. You are a clanwoman, and you are your mother's daughter. Never forget that."

When Elice still didn't move, Cinder sighed. "The Idarans believe you cannot directly control the field or the players on it, but you can manipulate them. The field has already been set, Elice, and you're going to have to learn to play the game of fire with a new set of rules and a different set of players."

Elice wanted to rail against her, wanted to scream that this was not some game, but a small part of her realized the truth to the other woman's words. A glittering, bitter cold washed through Elice. When she opened her eyes, frost fell around them, catching the light like a thousand sparks while Cinder watched in amazement. "I've always wanted to see snow."

Not bothering to correct the other woman, Elice pushed herself up. Her hands left damp prints on the frosty floor. That much power should have encased the room in ice, brought forth a blizzard with the power to bury an entire city. But with her eyes half closed, the falling frost could almost be mistaken for snow. That and Cinder's words brought a memory upon her.

It was the winter before Elice's father had died. He'd crouched before her, snow swirling gently around him. Her mother had circled them, her feet leaving a tamped down trail around them while she effortlessly negated any attempts Elice made to use her power.

Without winter, she was forced to fight hand-to-hand against her father, who was bigger and more experienced and so much stronger. He pinned her again and again and again, until she shouted, "What does it matter? If I ever have to fight in this cursed war, I'll just freeze them to death!"

Her mother paused in her circling. "And if ever you have to fight someone from the Summer Realm—if you ever face Nelay herself—your powers will be canceled out by hers." Elice saw her mother's dark frustration. Even at thirteen, Elice knew the two queens were so well matched that one might never defeat the other.

"Fighting isn't just about strength and experience—it's about your mind," her father added, ever the patient one. "You have to think, Elice. Have to outsmart your opponent. See the patterns in their movements and be ready to shift your strategy in a split second."

Elice dropped her head. "Strong as stone, supple as a sapling."

Her father had rested a heavy hand on her shoulder. "And more cunning than a queen."

Now, Elice's hand touched the belt, where the knife Storm had given her was carefully tucked away. Elice might not have access to her powers over winter, but she wasn't powerless. She could find a way to protect herself. She was, after all, her mother's daughter. The other players of the game might have more strength than she did, but she could manipulate them. She just had to figure out how.

Flanked by a pair of guards in vests and wide-legged pants, Elice and Cinder moved down a spiral staircase. At the bottom stood another set of guards who made no move to stop them. Elice stared at the palace towering above her. She didn't know what awaited her beyond it, but at least she would face it as a princess instead of a captive. She pulled out her necklace so the pendants would be visible.

"Thank you," she said softly to Cinder. "For everything." She started to walk, surprised when the woman continued by her side.

Cinder smiled. "You didn't think I'd let you face this alone."

Elice knew she couldn't fully trust Cinder, but neither did she consider her an enemy. "Can you come with me?"

"You'd be surprised what the queen's favorite seamstress gets away with."

The enormous palace loomed before them, a monstrosity of carved marble topped with golden onion domes. Elice and Cinder followed the guards up a wide set of stairs and approached enormous doors with phoenixes etched on the front and overlaid with beaten gold. More guards swung open the doors.

Elice froze. The way was kept clear by soldiers standing shoulder to shoulder, their faces stiff and unmoving. But behind the soldiers was an entire assemblage of Idarans, all with their dark features and foreign clothes. Silence rang like a struck tine, as if moments before the doors had opened the noise in the room had been deafening. At the end of the long line of soldiers, three thrones rested on a dais.

Thinking of the man who had attacked her with a knife, of his blood spilling into the street, Elice wanted nothing more than to run. "Why are there so many people here?" she asked in a hushed whisper.

Cinder leaned in. "Nelay may be an immortal, but she isn't invulnerable. Nor is her family. She needs the goodwill of the people. That means letting them see her triumphs."

Capturing me is the triumph, Elice realized. She glanced up, and her gaze landed first on Adar. She sucked in a breath to see him in such splendor, wearing bell-shaped trousers and a richly embroidered vest. A golden phoenix with spread wings dominated the banister above his head. Next to him was his mother, Nelay. Rycus sat beside her. Elice wondered where all of Adar's brothers and sisters were.

Cinder nodded to about two hundred women wearing bell-shaped trousers and fitted bodices. They seemed to be divided into two groups—one a mix of grown women, the other a mix of young women and girls. Elice thought she recognized Zahra's figure, but it was hard to tell with the robes. There was a proud tilt to the women's heads, and the way they held themselves bespoke grace and power.

"Priestesses," Cinder murmured. "The most powerful in the kingdom. Their High Priestess has almost as much power as Queen Parisa. Most of them can see the fairies."

Elice started. "So it is rare to see the fairies?"

Cinder raised a single brow. "There are very few who can see the world for what it is. Thankfully, I'm not one of them." She nodded to their right toward a group of older men and a few women. "The rest are lords, advisors, and professional guild leaders." Elice noticed most of them wore long robes, and scarfs wrapped around their heads.

She sensed something high above her and glanced up to see a wide walkway spanning the length of the room. Without any visible means to support itself, the walkway appeared as if it might collapse on top of Elice. Shaking the thought from her head, she turned her attention back to the three royals. She kept her gaze locked on the queen, refusing to acknowledge Adar at all as she and Cinder came to a halt just before the dais.

A herald's voice rang out with startling volume. "Elice, daughter of Ilyenna, who is Goddess and Queen of Winter."

In the silence that followed the pronouncement, Elice felt the sweat building on her skin even though she was surrounding herself with cold. She studied this queen—the woman who'd stolen her away from her dreams and locked her in a tower.

"Daughter of winter, is it true that you love my son?"

Elice's eyes widened and her mouth fell open, but no words came out. She hadn't been sure what to expect, but it was not this. She glanced helplessly at Adar, silently begging him to help her. He seemed to be trying to communicate something with his expression, but she couldn't understand.

"Why would you ask me this?" Elice finally said.

Nelay leaned back in her chair. "It is a simple question. Do you, or do you not, love my son?"

Elice wet her lips. "Why does it matter?"

Nelay's eyes glittered in the dark. "Right now, it's all that matters."

Elice's gaze swept over the room. Every eye was locked on her. She glanced down, staring at the mosaic on the floor—thousands and thousands of tiles that blurred together in an unrecognizable shape. Then she heard movement. She glanced up to see that Adar had risen from his throne and now descended the steps toward her.

"Adar—" Nelay said in a tone of warning.

He paused before Elice and took both of her hands in his. "I love you, Elice. You say you spent months in the darkness. So did I. It wasn't until I found you that I understood what true light is. For even in the darkness, you flourished. Like the prisms you made, you took what little light you were given and magnified it a hundred times, but with bursts of color." He reached up to cradle her cheek in his hand. "You add color to my life. And I would not part from you. Not ever."

He leaned forward and gently pressed his lips against hers. Elice forgot the crowds. Forgot the king and queen. There was only the warmth of Adar's kiss and his words, flooding out the doubts and fears, settling around her.

He pulled back, his gaze locked on hers. "Do you love me?"

"Yes." The word came easily, slipping from her mouth on a breath. For if she was a prism, he was the light that sparked through her.

Adar's smile grew until his whole face lit up with joy. "Thank you." He turned triumphantly to his mother. "I bargained for her life and won. Now you must let her live."

Elice gasped. "You mean if I hadn't said yes, she would have killed me?"

Adar squeezed her hand without looking at her. "I wouldn't have let that happen," he murmured.

Nelay watched them from her place on the throne. She took a deep breath and let it out slowly. "Very well, my son. I will let her live. But there is still the price you must pay."

"Adar!" Elice whispered. "You made a deal with her. You can't—you—"

"It's already done," Adar said before turning back to his mother. "I'm ready."

"The Balance is exacting, Son. Light and dark. Good and evil. Men and women. And in the end a life was spared, so another must be taken."

Adar closed his eyes. "I know"

Elice couldn't catch her breath. The room and all the people and the all guards with all their expressionless faces spun around her. She gripped Adar's vest. His hands came up and held her elbows, keeping her steady. "It will be all right," he told her.

Furious, Elice turned to the queen. "How can you do this? He's your son!"

Nelay clenched her jaw. "This was the only way—a life for a life."

"Elice, I made my choice," Adar said from behind her. "I knew the price. I paid it anyway."

She gripped his vest harder, crushing the embroidery beneath her fists. For days her heart had been shattered at his betrayal. Now she knew he had never betrayed her. He loved her. And she was going to lose him. He brushed back a lock of her hair. "You saved my life so many times, Elice. Now let me save yours."

He was just going to accept this? Accept dying and leaving her alone in this strange place, surrounded by her enemies? "No! I can't. I won't!"

"Elice—"

She pushed away from Adar and staggered toward the throne. Guards moved to intercept her, but Nelay held out a staying hand.

"Ask another price," Elice pled, standing before the Summer Queen. "Anything. But don't take him."

"I didn't set the price, child. The Balance did."

"But he's your son!"

"And he made his choice."

Elice's knees buckled and she hit the floor. She stared at the tiles beneath her, noticing they were bigger than she was, with darker veins running through the white, cool marble, which was polished to a shine so she could see her blurred shape, eyes wide, face bone-white. It was almost like ice.

Like . . . ice . . .

Tears blurred her vision. Around her fingers, swirls of frost spread out, curling protectively around her. In her desperation, she'd opened up her connection to winter so wide she thought it might kill her. But still, there was not enough power to do any damage. Cries of concern edged up from the crowd behind her, but the royals didn't seem afraid. "Please, I'm begging you," Elice said to the queen.

Nelay's gaze was unreadable. "Take her back to her tower and keep her there."

The guards started toward Elice. She staggered to her feet and pushed at one, but they gripped her under her arms and held her.

"Just let her go!" Adar cried. "Let her be free. Please, Mother."

"You bargained for her life, not her freedom, Adar." Nelay motioned to another set of guards. One of them drew his sword and started toward Adar.

"No!" Cinder screamed and lunged at one of them, but another guard snatched her, pinning her arms to her sides.

"Will you kneel on your own, Son?" Nelay asked without emotion. "Or will you be bound?"

Adar glanced back at Elice, his eyes full of love and sorrow. He nodded to her and then slowly got to his knees, his head bowed.

"Rycus! Stop her! Stop this!" Elice cried. But Adar's father only shot a nervous glance at his wife and remained silent. "Please!" Elice begged the guards who stood over him. "He's your prince! You know this is wrong!" But none of them would look at her. One of the guards raised his sword and poised it above Adar's neck.

"Another bargain!" Elice screamed. "My life for his! Please!"

"Stop!" Nelay's hand whipped up, palm out. The man with the sword paused.

"No, Elice, not after everything we've been through," Adar cried.

"My life for his." Elice spoke over him, her gaze locked on the queen. "Please."

Nelay sat back in her chair. "You really do love him, don't you?"

Tears filled Elice's eyes. "Yes."

Nelay nodded thoughtfully. "So you wish to take on his bargain?"

Adar was shouting now, the guards holding him back. Elice ignored him, her gaze solely focused on the queen. "Yes."

"A life for a life," Nelay murmured. "You accept these terms?"

"Yes," Elice said without hesitation. The air seemed to tighten around her like invisible bonds as the bargain was made.

Nelay sat back on her throne and motioned to the guards still holding Elice. "Very well, child. But the life I require is not yours."

"What?" Elice blurted. Adar stopped struggling and stared at his mother suspiciously.

Nelay pushed herself up from her throne. "You have bargained for his life, Elice, daughter of winter. And I have granted it. The price you must pay is this—you will destroy the Queen of Winter."

Elice made a squeaking sound, and her body went limp as though every bone had been crushed. The bargain had been sealed by the Balance. It would come to pass now regardless of what she might do to change it.

"You planned this all along, Mother," Adar said darkly. "You knew she would offer herself for me."

Nelay sighed. "If Elice truly loved you, she would sacrifice herself for you, just as you tried to do for her. That's what real love does. If not, she never really loved you at all and her execution would be set."

Adar struggled to be free of the guards, but they held him fast. One man struggled to put a manacle around the prince's wrist. "You never wanted my bargain—it was Elice you were after all along!"

"I'm sorry." His mother seemed to truly mean it.

"I won't go back," Elice said through gritted teeth. "I'll never see her again. And I'd kill myself before I ever hurt her."

Nelay regarded Elice sadly, and it seemed as if a great weight pressed down upon the Summer Queen, so heavy it almost crushed her for a moment. Her husband reached out and took her hand in his. Nelay seemed to draw strength from his grasp, for she inhaled deeply and straightened. "The Balance will see it is done." She motioned to her guards. "Take her back to the Winter Realm and let her go. Her mother will find her, or she will find her mother. Eventually." Nelay turned to leave.

"You sent Adar after me!" Elice shouted. "You tricked us both!"

Nelay turned back slightly. "I merely took the players and situations on the field and found a way to make them work to my advantage. It's what I do." She didn't say it proudly. More like it was a heavy burden to bear.

The guards started dragging Elice away.

Strong as stone, more supple than a sapling. The words came forcefully into Elice's mind. "And more cunning than a queen," she murmured to herself. She dropped, painfully yanking one arm free. She reached behind her clan belt, took the knife Storm had given her, and plunged it into the arm of the other guard holding her. He yelped, his grasp slackening. Elice wrenched the knife out of his arm and darted back toward the queen, then planted her feet and threw the dagger. Guards surged toward Elice, but she only watched the dagger, spinning end over end until it lodged up to the hilt in the center of Nelay's back. The queen crumpled.

Elice only had time for the barest of grim smiles before a guard plowed into her, slamming her so hard into the marble that her shoulder screamed in pain. She craned her head up, staring at Nelay.

Fire danced across the ground, rippling like water and melting the metal dagger. Blood gushed from the wound. "I can't move my legs!" Nelay cried as her husband reached for her.

Elice had severed her backbone. She'd healed enough animals to know that none survived a broken back.

A life for a life. If any life would pay the debt, why not Nelay's?

A dar saw the dagger hit his mother's back. He whipped his head around and caught sight of Elice trapped in a guard's arms, dark satisfaction in her gaze. Out of her line of vision, another guard raised his sword to strike her dead.

Adar reacted instantly, fire springing from his body. The guards holding him shouted and jumped back, their skin blistering. The guards around Elice became living pyres that screamed and clawed at their skin as if to pull off the fire. More guards rushed them. Adar lit every one of them on fire.

Then he dashed to Elice and took hold of her hand, knowing his fire wouldn't burn her if he didn't wish it to. Carefully, he encircled them in a different kind of fire—the same smokeless fire that made up his mother's wings. The halo of writhing flames felt like an extension of his own body.

The soldiers backed steadily away from the blaze, their commanders shouting at them to charge. A handful of soldiers tested the flames, and after their hands came away unhurt, the men charged.

"Don't!" Jezzel cried out. But it was too late. The soldiers' eyes went wide, their mouths gasping for breath. The flames did not burn, but they did smother. No one within the flames' reach could breathe, unless that person was touching Adar or his mother.

"Adar," Jezzel said. "Release them!"

Choking, the guards stumbled toward the open air. Adar's gut twisted, but he widened the perimeter, trapping the soldiers. "Let us go and I'll free them."

Jezzel stood over Adar's mother, blood dripping from her hands. She frowned but gave a curt nod. Adar retracted his fire, but he didn't extinguish it. Jezzel might be the commander of Idara's armies, but she was not above the law. And Elice had broken the highest of laws.

Adar pivoted, then hurried toward the west wing of the palace, Elice in tow. He kept his head up, looking for any dangers as the nimbus flared around them, driving away everyone before it.

"What is this?" Elice asked.

"We have to hurry." If his mother regained consciousness, she'd extinguish the flames. Holding Elice's hand, Adar pulled her along through the empty corridors of the palace. Their steps echoed off the hard floor. He shoved open the doors to the dungeons and, with Elice clinging to his hand, descended into the damp dark that smelled of sulfur and minerals.

"Where are we going?" she said from behind him.

"We'll never punch our way out of the city, even with my fire." Adar sent out a nimbus of blue fire that perfectly matched the fire in Elice's pendant. The nimbus illuminated the steps that led to a long tunnel lined with empty cells, the bars rusted. Suddenly the way opened to an enormous cavern. Adar sent the light up and intensified it. Jagged shadows elongated around them, clustering around the base.

But Adar could see the tunnel he was looking for. "It's an old luminash mine," he explained as they ran. "The temple was built here because of the proximity to the mines. The palace came later."

"Why doesn't the weight of the palace collapse the mine?" Elice managed to ask.

"The palace isn't built over it—the back gardens are." They reached the mouth of the tunnel. Adar extinguished the nimbus of fire and formed another before them. He kept it far enough away not to blind them, yet close enough to light their path as they ran headlong. Finally, they came upon what appeared to be a pile of rubble. Adar ran his hands along the surface.

"We're trapped," Elice cried. "You must have picked the wrong tunnel."

"All tunnels that lead to or from the palace were sealed up a long time ago." Adar finally found what he was searching for. He grasped the handhold, braced himself, and heaved. The pivot door opened, revealing more tunnel beyond. He shot Elice a grin over his shoulder. "You're not the only one who thinks secret passageways are a good idea."

She reached out to touch the door.

"It is plaster over wood," he explained, "but the men I hired did a good job making it look like the rocks around it." He turned and started jogging on.

"What were you afraid of?"

Although Adar didn't want to tell Elice the truth, it would be better than keeping secrets from her. "Your mother," he said. "I wanted a way to get my brothers and sisters out if she attacked the palace."

"If it was for your brothers and sisters, Adar, your family has to know it's there."

He set his mouth. "They do."

"So it's only a matter of time before they realize where we've gone."

"Right now, we're running from Idaran law more than my family."

For a time, there was only the sound of their footfalls, their ragged breathing. There were some twists and turns. A few times

Adar had to pause and study the markings painted on the sides of the tunnels. He kept a hard pace. After all, if he and Elice didn't disappear by the time the city guard came after them, it was over.

Finally, he stopped at one of the ladders. The tunnel continued on, but it wasn't maintained and Adar didn't know what lay beyond. He went up the ladder and found himself in a tack room. He pushed open the trapdoor, scattering hay and dirt that plumed up as the door landed with a crash.

He reached down and hauled Elice up just as the door to the room came open. The old man who stood there had a sword in hand, but he immediately sheathed it and bowed. "My prince, the gates of the city have been shut and there are soldiers on the parapets. What has happened?"

Adar thought quickly. Fleeing on horseback would be quicker and more nimble, but Elice didn't have the skills to ride. "We need a chariot," he told the old man. "And as many supplies as can be swiftly carried. When you're done with that, you and your men pair up, cover yourselves from head to toe, and scatter with the remaining chariots."

"But, sir, what if the rest of your family needs passage through—"

"That is an order," Adar growled.

"Stay here, my prince." The man spun on his heel and was gone.

"Where are we?" Elice asked as voices rose from beyond the wall.

Adar threw open a trunk labeled with the numeral 1. Inside was a variety of clothing and an array of weapons. He pulled out what he needed and donned the tan desert robes over his vest and pants. "When Thanjavar was sacked by the clanmen, my mother and what little remained of her people were trapped inside the palace walls. She thought it prudent to open a tunnel under the palace in case we ever had to get out. She secretly set up this waystation with supplies."

"Adar, your mother—"

"She'll be fine," he snapped. He opened the chest next to his, this one labeled with the number 2. He gathered up robes and daggers and pushed them into Elice's arms. "Nahid's robes should fit you."

He opened a secret panel, revealing an assortment of weapons, and took down a crossbow—he was terrible with a bow. When he turned back, he found Elice staring at the clothes as if she didn't know what to do with them. "Elice, you have to hurry."

She looked up at him, tears shining in her eyes. "Adar—I killed her."

Was that why she was being so withdrawn? "No, you didn't."

Elice hugged the stale-smelling robes to her chest. "The knife hit her spine. She won't survive that."

Adar pried the robes from her hands and settled them around her shoulders. "She will. Jezzel has refused her elice petal, so there's still one left."

"You mean I didn't kill your mother?"

He paused and looked at Elice, feeling like he was being torn in two. She'd tried to kill his mother—and would have succeeded if not for the elice blossom. But in her position, he had done the same. He tied the belt around Elice's waist and stepped back. "Do you really want her dead?"

"Do you want *my* mother dead?"

It was a fair question, but Adar didn't answer it. Instead, he reached into the second chest, pulled out a headscarf, and tossed it to Elice. "Put this on like Cinder showed you. Cover your face so only your eyes show. The fairies will have lost us in the tunnels. When they find us, they'll report our location back to my mother, who will be honor bound to tell the city guards." He tipped his head toward the wall of weapons. "Take anything you want."

Then he stepped out of the tack room and into the barn, which was manned by twelve men, all of them retired from the military due to injuries. The men had already prepared Adar's chariot. Four more were in various states of readiness, each pulled by a pair of swift desert horses bred for endurance. Packed in the chariots' bases were sacks of rations.

Adar stepped into the first chariot and took the reins in his hands. He turned as Elice, completely covered by the robes, climbed up beside him. He looked back at the men. "Draw away any attention and keep your identities hidden." The men would know what else to do—they'd been trained for this.

Adar slapped the reins across the horse's backs, urging them down the road that led away from the city. At the first decent road to the west, he turned toward the Razorback Mountains rising in the distance, while the other men continued on. They would split up later, taking main roads that led away from the city.

Adar looked back at Thanjavar. The setting sun lit up the gold onion domes of the palace. The gates were shut, and though he was too far away to spy them, he knew soldiers patrolled the wall. Adar wondered if he'd ever see his home again, or feel the cool embrace of the caves in the Adrack Desert. Ever see his brother and sisters.

All through the day, Elice watched the landscape blur past, with villages that thinned and grew progressively poorer and more run down. When night fell, Adar slowed the horses and started up a canyon that took them on a twisting path between ever-larger bare mountains, with only an occasional scrubby tree or some brush breaking up the stony ground. Soon, Elice's view of the stars was sliced into angles by the rise of the mountains.

Somehow she finally managed to sit down. But with the chariot rattling her brains out of her ears, she couldn't sleep.

Morning came on, cold and silent. In an exhausted daze, Elice kept reliving the memory of her knife spinning into Nelay's back. Of the curse the Summer Queen had laid upon her. Elice wasn't even sure what Adar thought running would accomplish. Even with the decoy chariots he had sent out, Nelay was sure to find them soon—she had too many fairy spies for them to avoid detection for long.

Just before mid-afternoon, Adar pulled the horses to a stop and looked down at Elice. "Time to get out." She wiped her eyes. It was strange to cry and have her tears not freeze on her cheeks. He crouched beside her and must have seen her tears. "Elice?"

"She cursed me to kill my own mother."

Adar's hands encircled her upper arms. "You can't kill her if you never see her again."

"But the Balance—"

"We'll find a way."

A part of Elice didn't believe him, but she firmly ignored that part. "How long before Nelay wakes?"

"Soon." He stepped down from the chariot. "She won't interfere with the bounty hunters that will be sent after us. She can't—her alliance with Idara is too important."

Thinking of the man who'd been beheaded, Elice shuddered. She unfolded herself, moved stiffly out of the chariot, and looked around. They were in some kind of abandoned village. Most of the roofs were gone, and some of the walls had tipped over or crumbled altogether. The place had long ago returned to the embrace of nature, the mountain reclaiming it as its own.

Elice lifted a hand to shield her sunburned face from the rays beating down on her. "Is it wise to stop? I mean, shouldn't we keep running—try to stay ahead of them?"

Adar was already backing the chariot into the gap left by a crumbled wall. "It would be suicide to push through the midday heat. Better to hide out now and move at night to conserve water until we reach the river."

"That's where we're headed? The river?"

Adar nodded. "See if you can find us somewhere protected to sleep."

Elice peered uneasily into a dark doorway. Inside, windows let in shafts of sunlight over sandy floors. If there had ever been furniture or bedding, time had long since turned them to dust. All that lingered now was the broken-down walls. She wondered what had happened to the people who had lived here. Why had they left, never to return?

The third building was cone shaped, so the roof was still intact. Elice had to crawl through the low doorway. Her fire pendant slipped out from her robes and offered just enough light to reveal scattering mice. She backed outside and turned to find Adar unhitching the horses.

"This should work," she called to him. He nodded as he buckled leather bonds around the horse's front legs. "What are you doing?"

He glanced at her. "They need to graze while we sleep. Hobbling them will keep them from going too far and allow us to catch them again."

She looked at the barren hills. "Graze on what?" He shrugged. "But what if wild animals attack them? They can't run."

He picked up the sack of provisions from where he'd set them on the ground. "Then they'll die."

Elice watched the horses lift their hobbled front legs and lunge forward to reach more grass. "I feel sorry for them."

Adar slipped past her, then crouched to step into the building. "An old smokehouse. Perfect. Too bad it doesn't come with a nice smoked ham." Elice didn't know what a smokehouse was, and she was too tired to ask. She crawled in after him.

He turned to stare at the opening, one hand raised. Even as she watched, smoke appeared on his palm in a thousand different shades of gray and brown. He chose each one, mostly tans, and wove them together over the opening, creating a wavering, self-sustaining smoke screen. When he was finished, it looked like a wall of old bricks. Elice could see the outlines of the world outside, but just barely.

"I didn't know you could do that." She moved to touch the smoke wall and then paused, shooting Adar a questioning look. He nodded. Her hand passed through, smoky curls spinning away from her touch. When she pulled back, the image re-formed.

"It wouldn't fool a person, but the fairies have no eye for such things." He gestured with a hand. "We can see out because of the sunlight, but they won't be able to see in. As long as I keep my connection open to summer, it will remain until I dispel it."

In awe, Elice studied him. "What else can you do?"

"Ah, the better question is what can't I do?"

She tried to smile.

"Weak, Elice." He turned away from her and rolled out a couple blankets in the center of the building, as if trying to avoid mice droppings. "I can make different kinds of fire—you saw that already." Adar held out his hand and a blue, liquid nimbus formed and slowly moved toward her. She shrank away as it came closer. "You can touch it. It won't burn you."

Elice reached out and the ball rested on her hand. It felt almost cool. "It's like the fire in my pendant."

"Yes. It gives light."

The blue slowly turned golden and writhed like a thousand snake tongues—just like the light that had surrounded Adar and Elice when they fled the palace. "The gold doesn't burn, but it

127

does snuff out the air," he explained. The golden light slowly turned into a red flame. "I'm not letting it burn you, but this kind of fire makes a smithy's furnace seem chilly." The flame shifted again, turning a blinding white that made Elice's eyes close. "The white light speaks for itself."

The light turned a vivid purple. "This last light—well, honestly, I'm not sure what it does." The fire shrank in on itself before disappearing completely, and Elice wished for the flames to come back.

She wiped her sweaty palms on her trousers. "What happened to this village?"

"The well probably dried up. It happens in these border towns."

"Couldn't they just get water from the river?"

"The nearest river is sixteen leagues from here." Adar opened up the provisions and removed some bread and dried meat. Without meeting her gaze, he held out some of both to her.

Suddenly, it was awkward. Elice sat next to him on the other blanket, as close to the opposite side as she could get. How could they ever reconcile the fact that their families were mortal enemies?

Finally, she could stand the silence no more. "Adar, I'm sorry. About everything." Asking for forgiveness for trying to kill his mother seemed unworthy, even tainted. But it was all she had to offer.

He stared out the open doorway and took a long drink from a water skin before handing it back to her. "It's ironic that you are named after the flower that saved my mother's life after you tried to kill her." He gave a forced laugh

The words were like a knife to Elice's chest. "By the Balance, when you say it like that . . ." Even though the water tasted like leather, she sucked it down until Adar pried it from her hands, saying something about conserving water.

He tore off a strip of bread, gave her half, and chewed on the other half. "Next time one of us decides to kill the other's mother, perhaps we should discuss it first."

"Adar . . ." She couldn't keep the pain from her voice.

"Really, Elice, I'm fine."

"No. You're not."

"What?"

"Whenever you're scared or hurt or angry, you make a joke out of it. It's how you deal with it."

He stared at her for a long time before closing his eyes tight. "She's my mother, and the woman I love tried to kill her. Do you know what that would do to me, to my father and my siblings . . ."

Elice opened her mouth to say something else, but Adar held out a hand to forestall her. "I understand, Elice, because I tried to do the same to your mother. It's just that loving my enemy's daughter is more complicated than I thought." Now he wouldn't meet Elice's gaze. "We should get some sleep. We're going to have to move out in the dark. If we push ourselves, we can reach the river by nightfall."

"What's your plan, then?"

"There are villages alongside the river. If we can hire a boat, we will move much faster and maybe even keep ahead of any bounty hunters. When we reach the coast . . ." Adar shrugged. "We'll figure it out from there."

They were silent for a time. "You never told me," she said. "About the time you were shot with a crossbolt."

He grunted. "Didn't I?" He drew up a leg, hooking his arm around it. "It was the first time I met Cinder—I was only twelve, but I insisted Darsam cart me along to rescue her. She'd been taken as a slave by the most notorious slaver in all of Idara."

Elice's mouth came open. "You helped rescue Cinder at twelve?"

"More like she rescued me. Twice, really. Once from the river after I was shot. The second time . . . there was a plot to kill my mother, and all the tribesmen who'd taken control of the government. If she hadn't warned us, I'm pretty sure the coup would have succeeded."

No wonder those Cinder and Adar has such trust in each other. "Isn't it a little ironic that a slave would save the country keeping her in bondage?"

His eyes met hers. "Because of Cinder, there isn't any more slavery in Idara."

12

When the worst of the heat had dissipated, Elice and Adar shared a meal of flatbread and prunes. The horses hadn't found any water and were listless and stubborn. Elice tried to draw some snow or ice in the hopes that it would melt and the animals could drink it. She managed a little, which she and Adar collected on a rock. But it was barely more than a mouthful for the poor beasts.

Adar didn't bother hitching up the horses, as the road didn't extend past the village. Instead, he helped Elice onto one of the animal's backs. She sat there, hands fisted in the horse's mane. Adar gently pried her hands free and put the reins in them. "Just keep yourself loose. Let your body move with the horse's."

The animal started out at a steady walk, and Elice found it wasn't as hard to stay on as she'd thought. They left the deserted village behind, the smoke image dissipating as they passed. She concentrated on freezing the miniscule amounts of moisture in the air and condensing it in the water skins. It took hours, but once she proved to Adar that she could replenish their water supply, he let her give most of it to the horses.

They moved on through the night, until sometime in the darkest hours when the horses refused to go on. Adar swung down and came back to help Elice. He removed the horses' bits and patted the animals' necks.

"What will happen to them?" Elice asked.

"If they manage to reach the river, they'll live." He swung the supplies over his shoulder and trudged on.

Elice lingered, looking at the magnificent beasts, whose heads now trailed the ground. For carrying her so far and so swiftly, she wished she had a better way to thank them than to leave them for dead. She reached out and ran her hand along the nearest horse's silky neck. Then she turned away and followed after Adar.

They trudged on through the rest of the night and morning. As the heat built, Elice tried to keep herself and Adar cool, but her connection to winter was like a wavering thread. Soon, her clothes were soaked with sweat, and even with her efforts to fill the water skin, it wasn't enough. She was desperately thirsty and hot. Adar seemed mostly unaffected, but he remained unusually quiet, and much of the time, their footfalls were the only sound.

Finally, at the sight of a grove of trees in the distance, Elice and Adar quickened their pace. But as they came closer, Elice realized with a sinking feeling that the trees were dead. Time had worn away the bark, leaving stark, skeletal branches scratching toward the sky. Still, they offered a smattering of shade and a little relief from the heat beating down on her face. Elice sighed as she stepped beneath their branches. They passed a pile of crumbled stones that might have been a dwelling once.

Adar's head swung from side to side. "There's one still alive."

Following his gesture, Elice saw a tree with a ragged roof of leaves, and a trunk in the shape of a three-sided "V." As she hurried forward, scattered dead leaves crunched under her feet and released an earthy musk. She rested her palm against the smooth trunk and closed her eyes, listening to the rustling of the leaves, and feeling the cool shade.

She pressed her nose to the bark and inhaled. "You said trees don't really have a smell."

"I did not!" Adar replied.

She rolled her eyes. "Yes, you did."

"I clearly remember—"

She held up her hand to silence him as she breathed deep. "This smells like spice and lemon and the pine trees of the Highlands." Elice hauled herself up into the branches and reached up to snap off a leaf. She broke it in half and held it under her nose. Bitter and fragrant. She looked up through the branches, marveling at the way the sky looked through the filter of green.

"This is a frankincense tree," Adar said from below her. He took his ice knife and scraped at the bark.

"What are you doing?" She moved down to sit in the tree's "V" and was now eye to eye with Adar.

He popped something in his mouth and then started scraping again.

"Adar, are you hurting this tree?"

He held out a strange yellow crystal. "Frankincense. Try it. It's good."

Elice took it and rolled it around in her fingers. It looked and felt like drips of candle wax. She set the crystal on her tongue. In an instant, pine and citrus filled her senses. As she chewed the frankincense, it gummed up her teeth. Then her mouth flooded with saliva and warmth—a warmth that slowly spread through her head and then her body.

Adar scraped off another chunk and held it in his hand. A little flame started in his palm, and the frankincense began to smoke. A wonderful fragrance filled the air, somehow reminding Elice of the Idaran palace.

"They burn this as incense at the temple," Adar said sadly.

She had never seen him so morose. "What's wrong?"

"I'm just tired." He crouched, picked up a flat rock, and tried to dig, but the ground was rocky and tightly packed. He tossed the rock and slumped with his back against the tree trunk, his upper arm resting against Elice's dangling ankle. "Water must have dried out here too—though there must be a little for this tree to survive. But the roots go deep, and without a shovel to dig with . . ." His voice trailed off. "Doesn't matter. It's not that far to the river. We should reach it by nightfall." He held up the water skin and let her drink most of her half, only leaving a little in reserve. "You want to eat?" he said.

Elice leaned back and stared up through the leaves. She was cradled inside a tree that seemed to conform to her body. She pulled from winter, surrounding herself and Adar with a bit of cool air. After the turmoil of the last few weeks, she could finally relax. She drifted to sleep, and when she woke the light was intense, streams of it pushing down on her closed eyelids. She squinted at the glaring sunlight that filtered down on her through a shifting, rustling shadow.

She sat up a little, her neck stiff. Adar was walking toward her from the direction of the crumbled building. He handed her some bread and dried meat, then tore off pieces of frankincense and collected them in his hand. "Not much farther is the head of the river Sindhu. Plenty of water, and we can both bathe."

"What if the bounty hunters show up?" Elice asked.

"I'll burn them."

She remembered the living pyres when they escaped Thanjavar. "We have to flee Idara and find somewhere else to live. I have family with the clanmen—"

The frankincense in Adar's hand began to smolder. "They'd kill me the moment we stepped onto their land."

She scooted to the edge of the tree and rested her fingers lightly on his arm. "The highmen then. We could both use our powers in Svass."

Adar dropped his head. "You don't understand."

"Then tell me." Elice fought to keep her voice even. He'd been sullen and moody all day. She missed his jokes and teasing.

His shoulder rose and fell in a silent sigh. "A life for a life—you heard my mother. If you don't go back to the Winter Queendom and kill her, you'll die. It might be in an accident. It might be from some sickness, but your life will be forfeit."

Elice reeled back. "But you said—"

Adar spun around, the incense falling from his hand. "I lied."

She stared at him and slowly shook her head. "I can't kill my own mother."

He moved to stand in front of Elice. "Even to save your life? Save the world?"

She crossed her arms. "Could you?"

"If there was no other choice." He raised haunted eyes to Elice's, and she finally understood his silence all day. One way or another, he was convinced he was going to lose her.

"You don't understand," she told him. "It's my fault. The war, the failed peace negotiations, my mother's unending hatred. All of it." She told him about how her father had died, how she had caused it.

Adar listened patiently, and when she was finished, he took her hand. "Listen to me, Elly, you didn't force your mother to assign blame where none existed. And you didn't consume her with hatred. She did that herself."

Elice felt a deep tremor, almost as if releasing a little of the guilt let her relax a muscle she'd been holding taut for far too long. "I won't return to the queendom." If she never saw her mother again, there was no way she could kill her. The incense began catching the leaves scattered on the ground on fire. Elice ignored it. Adar had power over fire. It would cease to burn if and when he wanted it to. "The bounty hunters?"

"I'm not worried about them," Adar said. "I just had to get you away long enough for the word to reach your mother. When she comes for you, you have to go with her."

"I already told you, I can't do that."

"Elice, no matter what happens, I trust you to do the right thing."

She leaned forward and placed a hand on his chest. She was aware of the flames licking up her legs, but they did not burn her. Instead, they felt like the light caress of wavering silk. "Even without the bargain I made, I would never go back there. I might be safer, but I would never be happy."

Adar closed his eyes and leaned forward. "What if I came with you?"

She reached up and cradled his cheek in her hand. "Then you would never be happy either. There's nothing there for either of us."

The flames licked up the tree, but the bark did not burn, and neither did the leaves. Elice was surrounded by the nimbus of fire. It felt hot, yet pleasant. She did the only thing she could. She placed gentle kisses on his mouth, her fingers skimming over the stubble on his head. He froze, his mouth coming open a little as if in surprise.

Then he leaned into the kiss, his lips moving expertly against hers, his arms wrapping around her. Her skin was burning, like when she'd stood too close to the bonfire and the heat had beat against her face. Adar even tasted like fire—flame and light and ash. Elice felt a delicious heat rolling through her, leaving her head and toes tingling.

And then Elice wrapped her legs around him. His breath hitched in his throat and his kisses grew desperate and hungry. The heat roared to life, flames licking around her skin like a thousand ribbons of silk. His hands worked at the tie of her robe, opening it to reveal the silk dress she still wore from days before. She didn't think it was possible, but his desperation increased and he kissed her as if he'd never kiss her again.

Suddenly there was a clap of thunder. Adar pulled back, hauling Elice out of the tree. They both looked at the dirty blue sky with no cloud in sight. The flames vanished as if they'd never been, leaving Elice cold and aching. A sudden bolt of lightning split the sky, slamming down on one of the skeletal trees. Elice screamed, but the sound was swallowed up in the crash of the lightning bolt. The tree split in half and was devoured by flames. Adar held out his hand and the fire disappeared, leaving behind a wisp of smoke and the charred cinders at the heart of the split tree.

Elice realized she was clutching his arm, but she couldn't let go. "Your mother?"

Breathing hard, he stared at the burned tree. "The Sundering."

Without another word, he turned to her, gently pulled her robes closed, and tied the sash. "Come on. There isn't much time left." He was already moving, tightening the straps of his baldric and checking the knives strapped to his body.

"What do you mean to do?"

"We'll head downriver. About a half day's ride north is a small town. We can purchase a boat to take us to the sea."

13

At a small village, Adar traded some coins for a sturdy raft and some supplies. Elice was pretty sure the old man he traded with had taken advantage of them, but there were no other options. While Adar worked the pole, Elice trailed her hands and feet in the sharp cold of the water, feeling more at home than she had in weeks. She fell asleep that way, and when she woke, it was almost night.

Adar showed her how to work the pole, and he took his turn sleeping while she kept them to the center of the ever-widening river. The mountains became steeper and more rugged, until the raft floated through a gorge so deep the sky was halved on both sides by the massive walls of the canyon.

Farther on, they saw another village, this one built into recesses in the cliffs. Dogs barked as the boat drifted by. By morning, Elice could make out a few herds of sheep and a shepherd boy watching them in silence. She and Adar spent the entire day on the raft, eating and watching the landscape slip past.

It was almost night again when they reached a little cove. Adar and Elice strained to haul the raft ashore, and they made a meal of dried meat and fruit. In the quiet that followed, Elice could hear a rhythmic rushing above the sound of the river.

She rose to her feet. "I know that sound."

"The ocean," Adar said, and she realized he'd known it was there all along.

On the other side of the alcove, Elice pushed through the brush that grew thick around the water. Now she could see the sea. She crossed the sandy dunes and came to stand on the shore, watching the sun sink beneath the horizon, painting the water in gold.

The light made her eyes sting and water, but the ocean, even if it was brilliant blue instead of black, seemed like home. She took a few steps forward and felt the waves crash against her feet, the sand shifting beneath her as she sank.

"Elice," Adar said quietly from behind her. "We're too exposed out here."

She left the sea reluctantly, the sand sticking to her damp legs and between her toes. In the alcove, she and Adar wedged themselves under an outcropping of rock. He set up a sort of lean-to at the opening and settled a warm red fire that hovered above the ground, taking the chill from the air. Not that the chill bothered Elice, but the warmth was rather pleasant. She fell asleep in Adar's arms, the steady beat of his heart thrumming next to hers.

Adar woke with a shiver and sat up. His breath clouded the air. His gaze went immediately to his red fire, but it was burning just as hot as when he'd fallen asleep. He carefully lifted Elice off his chest, which she was using as a pillow, only to discover that his left arm felt like a dead weight. He shifted the blankets to keep Elice covered, then pushed himself up with his right arm. His left arm tingled as the sensation came back.

He peered out of the lean-to, his breath catching at what he saw. A half dozen frost fairies, their bodies glimmering a pale blue, darted about the alcove, weaving back and forth over the world, leaving a trail of frost in their wake.

Adar knew what this meant. Fire and ashes, he didn't want to face it. But it didn't matter what he wanted. It never had. He glanced out once more, hoping against hope that his eyes had deceived him. Though the fairies were gone now, the frost they'd left behind continued to expand.

What froze him in his tracks was the dark figure standing beside the river. All Adar could make out was the outline of a cloak, but he didn't have to see her face to recognize his mother. With one glance back at Elice, he slipped out of their makeshift shelter and strode out to meet his mother, anger burning his tongue. But when he saw her dark eyes glimmering in the starlight, his words snuffed out.

"Adar, I'm sorry," she murmured.

Surprised, he stopped short. "For deceiving me or for making such a cruel bargain?"

"Both," Nelay said immediately.

"And you just expect me to forgive you?"

The wind picked up, tugging at her cloak. "No," she said evenly. "I've lost you. I had to accept that before we began. But Adar, I had to. Please understand."

He could smell a storm coming. "There has to be another way. Peace can—"

"No," Nelay said sharply. "I have tried every other way for twenty years. This ends, and it ends tonight." Her voice softened. "But I will try to end the curse myself. I will try to spare your Elice that much grief."

Adar jerked his head up. "You still plan to kill Ilyenna?"

His mother's half grin was illuminated by the distant flash of lightning. "I was very careful in the wording of my bargains. 'I will deliver the killing blow myself.' That was my first bargain, the bargain with you. The second bargain—'You yourself will destroy the Queen of Winter.' Well, Elice has lured her mother here. Let's hope that's enough."

"What if it isn't enough?"

Nelay's mouth tightened. "That's why I did all of this. One way or another, Ilyenna will be destroyed."

Now Adar could see that his mother wore armor beneath her cloak. The bulges behind her shoulders suggested she had her swords as well.

"My going to the Winter Queendom in the first place, falling in love with Elice, me overhearing you and Jezzel—you orchestrated it all?"

Nelay chuckled. "What did you expect? You've known all along that I'm the greatest strategist to have ever lived. Though I will admit, I didn't expect you to love her. That had me scrambling to rework the plan."

Adar felt a moment's relief that Elice might have escaped her fate, but the relief was followed by a stab of guilt that the cost was her mother dying. "So you never intended to execute Elice."

Nelay sighed. "She's too valuable to die."

Looking back at the shelter, he realized pain awaited Elice either way. He turned to face Nelay again. "Then don't fail, Mother. I can't bear to see Elice kill her." Even as the words left Adar's lips, he knew Elice might never forgive him. Not for arranging the death of her own mother.

Nelay took his face in his hands and kissed his forehead. "I have tried to love you, my son. Tried harder than you can ever know."

Tix alighted on her shoulders. "My queen, it's time," the fairy said in her sticky spider voice. Nelay's wings flared out from under her cloak in a deep blue fire that cast only a little light. She took to the sky, Tix riding on her shoulder.

"Adar?" came Elice's breathless voice. He spun around, wondering guiltily what she'd heard. She pushed past the lean-to. "Something woke me. A bright light that—" She froze, no doubt noticing the frost gleaming around them. "She's coming." Distant flashes of lightning revealed her facing north with a hard expression.

Should Adar tell her that a battle between their mothers was looming, and that it was better for the world if Ilyenna died? Before he could decide, Elice ran headlong toward the edge of the alcove. He hurried after her. "What are you going to do?"

"She's coming for me. After all I did to her, she risked everything to come for me." By the sound of Elice's voice he could tell she was crying, or close to it. "Don't you see, Adar? That means she is capable of love! Perhaps there can be peace after all."

He didn't believe it. Not after all the years of hatred and death. He caught up to Elice and pulled her into his arms. Fire and burning, he'd been so angry when she'd hurt his mother. And now he was doing the same thing to Elice by letting his mother kill hers. But what else could he do? If he warned Elice, she'd put herself in harm's way. "It's going to be all right." Adar hated himself even as the lie left his lips.

A distant boom echoed off the sides of the cliff. Elice's head whipped around. "Nelay," she breathed, her voice full of fear. She wrenched herself free of Adar's arms and rushed forward. He followed her.

Out over the black ocean, the clouds were stained a blood red and a poisonous green that emanated from two sets of wings, the figures at their center rushing each other. Nelay dodged a shaft of ice and lunged, slicing through Ilyenna's wings. Ilyenna tottered for only half a moment, before she spun, her damaged wings wrapping around her body as she dropped from the sky, Nelay a beat behind her. Ilyenna plunged into the water like a stone, turning the waves a lurid green that spread even as lightning flashed.

Nelay tried to follow but slammed into a sheet of perfectly clear ice. She lay there for a moment, dazed.

"No," Adar cried.

Ilyenna broke through, her axe plunging toward Nelay, but then his mother kicked upward. They collided, rolling together over the iced-over sea. Where the colors from their wings met, gold light shimmered and sparked. The light grew brighter and brighter until Adar could see neither of them. He turned away, his hands outstretched to shield himself.

The wind howled, gusting so hard it nearly pushed him over. He staggered against it, reaching for Elice with the intention of hauling her to safety. But the wind blew something into him and his knees buckled. He lay on the ground, stunned. Able to see, but unable to move.

"Adar!" Elice screamed as she dropped beside him. He struggled to roll over, but his movements were sloppy and uncoordinated. The ground beneath them bucked violently, and she draped herself protectively over him. He muttered something but she couldn't hear it over the rush of the wind. "What?"

"Alcove," he managed, pointing. It was obvious he wanted her to go back there, but it wouldn't be any safer—not if tremors caused rocks to fall. Then his eyes rolled up and he slipped into unconsciousness.

Elice touched the lump on the side of his head. It was bleeding, but she thought he'd be all right. She looked back at her mother, wishing she could do something, anything to help her win the battle with Nelay. Out of mere habit, Elice opened herself to winter and was shocked to feel it flooding through her.

Her gasp was ripped away by the wind. She let the cold seep into Adar's head to help with the pain and swelling. Then she pushed herself to her feet and held her hand over him, forming a hard, thick layer of ice around him.

She turned from him and let a shield fill one hand, a spear the other. Protected behind her shield, she strode up the sand dune, testing the weight of the spear in her hand and waiting for an opening to launch it at Nelay.

Her mother and the Summer Queen had broken apart, and the light was red and green again. The tremors seemed to settle, and the wind died down enough that Elice dared lower her shield a fraction. Nelay rushed toward the shore. Elice shifted her stance and cocked her arm back.

But as the Summer Queen passed over her, Elice hesitated. There had to be another way. "Nelay!" she shouted. "We can end this. We can find peace!" Nelay's eyes locked on Elice, fury burning in her gaze, but she flew on and disappeared over the mountain ridge.

"Elice!" Ilyenna cried. She pivoted midair and dove toward Elice, arms outstretched as if to snatch her from the shore and carry her off to safety. Ilyenna couldn't see the army that rose up behind her. Couldn't see them draw back their bows. Couldn't see them launch a volley that blacked out the stars.

"No!" Elice cried. She formed an ice shield to protect her mother, realizing a beat too late that she wouldn't have time to make one for herself. Elice tensed for the coming pain, but something barreled into her and slammed her backward onto the sand. Arms held her, pinning her down. Her mouth was full of sand. She spit it out, blinking furiously and gasping for breath.

Then the arms went slack. She twisted to find Adar on top of her, his expression grim. "Adar?" she gasped.

He groaned, his face red and the veins standing out. She glanced back at the ice she'd encased him in. One side had a large hole. Adar had melted his way out.

Elice suddenly realized she was wet and looked down to see blood soaking her robes. She searched for any signs of pain.

Nothing. It wasn't her blood. Her gaze went back to Adar in horrified understanding. "No," she cried.

She scrambled out from under him and saw the arrows sticking out of his back, three of them, two in his lower back and one at his shoulder. "No!" Her hands reached for the arrows, determined to stop them from hurting him. But then she froze. Taking them out would only kill him faster. "No!" she screamed again.

Hands gripped her and pulled her to her feet. She recognized the cold grasp even as she turned. "No," she wailed to her mother. "You have to save him! Do something!"

Ilyenna took hold of Elice, her wings rising for a down stroke that would take her to the queendom, where Elice would never see Adar again. "No!" Elice screamed again, tears running down her hot face. She wrenched herself free and stumbled back. "He cannot die! I love him!"

"We have to go before she comes, Elice." Her mother's hands stretched out imploringly. "My strength is already waning. We must return to the queendom before it leaves me completely."

Elice crouched beside Adar. He was very still, his eyes tracking hers. "A life for a life," he said breathily. "You're free."

Was he paying the price of her bargain? Elice gently brushed the sand from his face. "Don't. Don't leave me."

He only smiled at her. "You were worth it."

"Don't talk like you're dying."

Ilyenna knelt and grasped Elice's shoulders. "Come, we must go. The boy is dying. And if we stay here any longer, so will we."

"Elly, go!" Adar said.

From behind them, a scream echoed off the cliffs. Ilyenna's gentle hands turned to steel as she darted to her feet and shoved Elice behind her. "Winter fairies, to me. Defensive formation."

The fairies circled around Ilyenna and Elice as Nelay shot to-ward them, streaking through the sky like a comet.

Ilyenna formed an ice spear, but it shattered in her grip. Staring grimly at it, she clenched her jaw. Elice reached for the magic and found only a trickle. The rest was locked up far, far to the north.

"Run, Elice," her mother ordered, even as she turned to face her foe.

But Nelay didn't charge them. Instead, she dropped beside her son, her scream turning to a wail of grief so sharp it seemed to tear the world in two. Her wings went out in a puff of smoke as she stroked Adar's face, murmuring to him. Ilyenna watched for a moment and then strode forward, forming a needle-like dagger and poising it to strike.

Elice pulled on her arm. "Leave them alone, and I'll come back to the queendom with you."

"Let me go, Elice," her mother hissed below her breath, "and we can end this once and for all."

"No!" Elice pushed her way between the two women. "I'll fight you myself if I have to."

Nelay raised hollow eyes to her immortal enemy. With a wave of her hand, she melted the knife in the Winter Queen's grasp. "Your power is spent, Ilyenna. What other price must we both pay before this is over?"

When Ilyenna didn't answer, Nelay formed a ball of fire in her hand. Elice darted protectively in front of her mother. "Don't!"

Nelay's gaze softened a fraction. "It will be easier this way, child. I promise you."

Elice shook her head. "The bargain has ensured this will happen, one way or another. But not like this."

Nelay's expression was uncertain, but the ball of fire faded to nothing. Ilyenna let out a gasp of disbelief even as Elice dropped to the ground beside Adar. She pressed her fingers to his throat. "His heart still beats!" She hauled off her bloody robes and ripped the linen, using it to pin his arms together so he wouldn't move and further injure himself. She gripped Nelay's shoulders with bloody hands. "There has to be another petal." Nelay could only shake her head. "Then you have to take him to the healers in Thanjavar."

The Summer Queen shook her head harder. "I can't carry him that far. My arms aren't strong enough."

"You have to try." Elice bit her lip, forcing herself to think. And she remembered the way the horses' saddles had been tied. "We'll strap him to you."

Nelay nodded. Elice got under Adar and helped to push him up. His mother tried to hold him up, but he outweighed her and she struggled to keep him from slipping, a slip which would probably kill him.

"Mother, help us," Elice begged. To her shock, her mother did, holding Adar in place while Elice tied the strips. Between the three of them, they managed to tie him to Nelay.

Ilyenna stepped back, blood on her pristine robes. "This isn't over Nelay," she said darkly.

"But it will be soon. One way or another," Nelay replied. Then she spread her fire wings, gave Elice a grim nod, and shot into the sky.

Elice watched them go. In the silence following the chaos, dread filled her to overflowing. But her attention was pulled away from the fading red sky to the light catching off the weapons of the Immortals as they started down the hill toward them.

"It is long past time we left this place," said the Winter Queen.

For once, Elice didn't argue.

Elice wandered around her room. Everything was exactly as she'd left it. But she looked over the reliefs in the walls with new eyes, recognizing from her own memories the mountains and meadows of the Shyle, with Shyleholm resting in the center.

She walked out onto her balcony, her fist clasping the pendant Adar had given her. She could feel the radiating cold and the gentle lick of the flames as she stared out over the vast, frozen landscape. It was a harsh beauty, full of subtle colors and sharp angles. Surprisingly she had missed it—missed the smell of snow, and the prisms' reflection off her trees.

Behind her, she heard the bedroom door creak open. "Elice?"

She turned at her grandfather's voice. Ilyenna stood behind him, her hands folded in front of her. Elice met the old man's watery blue gaze. His face had aged ten years in the few short weeks they'd been apart. He hurried into the room and gathered her into his arms. "The boy?"

"She told you?"

"Yes, everything."

"I don't know if he yet lives," Elice managed, her voice breaking.

Her grandfather let out a heavy sigh. "Sorrow is a bitter drink. Would that you had not had to taste it."

Elice turned her face into the wind, letting it freeze the tears on her cheeks. "I have something to tell both of you, about Storm."

Otec's brow furrowed. "My sister?"

"And Holla." Elice quickly explained all that had befallen her grandfather's sisters since they were taken as slaves by the Idarans. Before long, tears lined his weathered cheeks.

"Storm wanted to tell you that she forgives you for leaving her," Elice said finally. "Every day she forgives you."

He bowed his head. "If only I could forgive myself."

"If you hadn't done what you did, the clans would have fallen," Ilyenna said as gently as she ever said anything.

Her words resonated deep within Elice. If she didn't kill her mother, the Sundering might destroy the entire world. Trembling, Elice took her grandfather's gnarled hand in hers and placed in it the half-beaver carving he'd given to his sister all those years ago. He stared at it for several seconds, then pulled out its match and held the two pieces together to make a whole at last. "The Balance has brought me full circle. And you too, Elice, for now you are where you began."

"Yet everything has changed," she whispered.

Her grandfather rested both his hands on the top of his cane. "I had to choose. That choice meant I betrayed my family for the good of my people. Your mother had to make a similar choice once. Now, so do you."

Elice gaped at him, wondering if somehow he knew the decision before her.

"What choice is that?" Ilyenna asked icily.

"It's the kind we all have to make—to let go of something so we can hold onto something else." Otec turned angry eyes to his daughter. "Rone fought once, fought for the woman he loved. Nearly killed himself twice trying to save her. You did the same for him. As did I for Matka. Do you think to deny your daughter that same right?"

Elice sagged a little as she realized her grandfather meant fighting for love. But wasn't that the same thing? She had to choose. Choose between saving the world or her mother. And in the end Elice could lose both.

Ilyenna's jaw clenched. "Have you forgotten that Adar lured Elice from the safety of the queendom? As a result, she was imprisoned and sentenced to death. Do you truly think she can choose to go back?"

No. Elice had to convince her to make peace. There was still light in her. Elice just had to make her see it. "You are a quarter Idaran, Mother."

"Is that the lie the Idarans told you?" Ilyenna scoffed. "The first time Raiders came, they killed or enslaved your grandfather's entire family. The second time, they took me. They did—" she faltered "—unspeakable things. So the clans rose up against Idara, determined to make sure they could never hurt our people again. That Summer Queen, the woman you call Nelay, wiped them out, to the very last man. Whole generations, gone. No mercy. Gone. Your grandfather lost his only son and many of his grandsons in that war. I lost nephews and old friends. Do not think for a moment that we carry any of their tainted blood."

Elice met her grandfather's haunted gaze. "An Idaran didn't tell me. Storm did."

"Storm?" Ilyenna said, her gaze flicking between her father and her daughter.

Otec sighed heavily. "Matka—your mother—was half highwoman, half Idaran."

"She was an Idaran slave," Ilyenna retorted. "You told me that yourself."

"It's more complicated than that," Otec murmured after a pause. The wind picked up, gusting across the balcony in erratic bursts. "I never told you. We never told anyone. It would have meant Matka's life if anyone had found out the truth. And after she died . . ." Otec paused, his voice hitching. ". . . you already hated the Raiders—everyone did. I didn't want you hating your mother, too."

Ilyenna swept the loose hair away from her face. "This can't be true."

Feeling battered by the wind, Elice took a step toward her, hand outstretched. "Don't you see? This war is tearing us apart. Seek peace with Nelay—she will give it to you. Adar and I . . ." Her voice broke. *Adar could very well be dead by now.* She shook the thought from her head. *No, he has to be alive.* "Adar and I will marry, and the queendom and the realm will know peace. We can stop the Sundering, and—"

"There's no such thing as the Sundering," Ilyenna cried. "Ridiculous stories to lure us into another trap!"

"I've seen it!" Elice said.

Her mother turned away. Elice reached for winter and formed an ice dagger in her hand. Gusting harder now, the wind pushed her hair back from her face and blew what looked like swirling columns of fallen leaves. But there were no leaves in the Winter Queendom.

"Let's go inside. A storm's brewing." Otec eyed his daughter as he said this, clearly blaming her wild emotions.

But something wasn't quite right about this storm. Letting the knife dissolve, Elice stepped to the rail of the balcony as the wind blew one of the leaves toward her. The shape was too curved for a flat leaf. She leaned as far over as she could, caught it in her cupped hands, and brought it to her face. It was not a leaf but a cold fairy, the most common and plain of the fairies, with simple features—angular eyes and a pointed nose, chin, and ears. The fairy wore a misty dress. Her wings warped the light, making the air seem to shift and bend strangely.

But the fairy wasn't moving. Something was wrong with her. Elice blew on the creature, but that didn't wake her. *Strange. Fairies don't get sick.* Shielding the creature from the wind with her hands, she hurried inside. She settled the fairy on her table.

Otec trailed Elice into the room and sat heavily in the chair. "What's wrong with her?" He gently prodded the fairy.

"She's dead," a hollow voice said from the balcony. "I didn't notice it before—I thought it was just my anger. Didn't realize it was death." Ilyenna stared out over the queendom, her face as hard as the carved statues in Elice's forest.

"Fairies cannot die unless *you* kill them," Otec protested.

Ilyenna turned. Her gaze snapped to her father and then to Elice. Dozens of war fairies streamed toward the Winter Queen. "Hundreds of them died," Ilyenna said, her face expressionless. "All at once. Dropping from the sky."

That meant all those blowing leaves were actually dead fairies. "It's the Sundering, Mother. You have to believe it now. You have to stop this."

"This is the Summer Queen's doing," Lowl growled as she came within range, her lieutenants yipping their agreement.

Elice huffed. "How could she kill fairies in the heart of winter?"

Lowl turned glowing yellow eyes on her, and Elice remembered how the fairy had grinned at her, blood dripping from her fangs when she'd attacked them on the mountain pass. The hair stood up on the nape of Elice's neck.

"What other explanation is there?" Lowl spat out.

"Mother." Elice came up beside her, knife in hand. If she couldn't convince her . . . "I've tried to tell you, the Sundering —"

Her mother pulled away. "Winter and summer have always battled! It is the way of the queens."

Elice shook her head. "Not like this. Squabbles over territory during spring and summer—not pitting your powers against each other. When you fought each other over the ocean, your green light met her red and created white light so intense I couldn't keep my eyes open. The ground began to tremble and shake."

"That was hours ago," Lowl protested. "And the damage never reached the queendom."

Elice wet her lips. "What if the effect is like a ripple? It takes longer to reach faraway places and when it does, it's weaker."

"Ilyenna, I think you should listen to her," said Elice's grandfather from his place at the table.

Ilyenna's gaze seemed uncertain as she looked from Lowl to Elice and back again. A sprig of hope blossomed inside Elice. Then one of the counselors, Ursella, gasped and began to struggle. Ilyenna whirled toward the fairy—one of the original ones who'd chosen her—and held out her hand. The fairy collapsed onto her palm, the fans of frost at her back beginning to wilt. "My queen," she said in a tinny voice.

"Ursella?" Ilyenna cried. "What is happening?"

"The magic," Ursella said even as she rolled over, her silver hair fanning across Ilyenna's palm. "The magic is slipping away."

Another fairy zipped through the door—it was Tanyis, her wings like broken glass. "The fairies most vulnerable to heat are fading first, my queen," she reported. "The cold fairies are already dead. The frost fairies are sickening. My ice fairies are weak."

"Just like how we feel when the Summer Queen is near," Lowl said, pointing south. "This is her doing. It has to be."

"No!" Elice cried. "It's the Sundering!" By the Balance, why couldn't they see?

Ilyenna's gaze was fixed to the south. "I do not feel the Summer Queen within our borders, Lowl."

Elice stormed in front of the general. "You're a warmongering dog, slavering for hot blood and flesh between your teeth."

Lowl tipped her head and glared at Elice, then looked at her mother. "I have commanded your armies for forty years, my queen. Have I ever counseled you false?"

"You have yet to win this war," Elice shot back.

But Ilyenna didn't appear to be listening to either of them. She was staring at the fairy in her hands. Ursella's eyes were open but sightless. "She was one of my oldest friends," Ilyenna mumbled.

"Chriel was one of your oldest friends too," Elice reminded her. "She tried to warn you this was coming. You didn't listen."

Ilyenna lifted haunted eyes to Elice. "Nelay sends her son to my queendom to lure away my daughter, then passes a death sentence on her head, and you expect me to believe some wild story from a rumor of dead legends?"

Elice took a step toward her. "It's the truth behind the tales, Mother. The—"

"It is fiction!" her mother roared, slamming a wave of cold into Elice. Ilyenna held up Ursella's limp body as proof. "This is reality." Tears fell from Ilyenna's eyes as she gently set the fairy's blue corpse on the table. Otec came up beside his daughter to rest a weathered hand on her shoulder.

Elice took first one step toward her mother, then another, an ice knife forming in her hand. She gripped the hilt so hard her fingers were numb. She lifted the knife, staring at the spot between her mother's shoulder blades. She thought of the world—not just Idara but Svass and the clanlands. But then she remembered what Chriel had always said—"Outshine the darkness." And Adar had called her a prism, breaking the light into fire and color.

Elice's hand fell, the knife turning to a dusting of snow that sifted from her fingers. "You won't do it."

Her mother turned to her, tears frozen in tracks on her cheeks. "What?"

"You will see the chaos and death and destruction, and you will understand that the Sundering is real. You won't destroy the world. You can't. Because there is too much light in you."

Frowning, Ilyenna stepped onto the balcony and looked back as the wind twisted her dress around her legs. "I will not return, not until this is over. One way or another. Lowl, to me." Ilyenna stormed out of Elice's room, followed by the fairies.

Elice stared at the bodies on her table. A cold fairy and a frost fairy—those whose magic was most tied to that of winter.

The Sundering was upon them.

15

With a feeling of dread, Elice watched the sun slip toward the horizon. Had she made a mistake in letting her mother live? Had she trusted in something that wasn't there?

"Tell me about my grandmother," Elice said to her grandfather, trying to remember that two foes could find a way to coexist, even to love each other. "Tell me about the woman who was your enemy."

"Her mother was a slave from the Highlands," Otec began, his voice tired and rough. "Her father was her Idaran master. She was taken to the temple as a girl, as soon as they realized she had the Sight. She came to the clanlands to gather information for a book on healing remedies. I took her into the mountains to look for a flower." He looked at the pendant hanging from his granddaughter's neck. "The elice blossom."

He stopped for a moment, his throat working, and then he went on. "It was while I was gone that the Shyle was attacked."

Elice had never known her grandmother, who had died when Ilyenna was young. "After she betrayed you, you fell in love with her anyway?" Just like Adar had betrayed Elice.

156

Her grandfather nodded. "Not at first. But she risked everything to help me. And she loved me. After the invasion was over and my family was all gone, she was the only happiness left for me."

Elice gripped the banister, her fingers blanching white. "I feel that way about Adar." Beneath her hands, she sensed a vibration running deep through the palace. She looked out over the landscape, at her tinkling and shuddering ice forest.

Her grandfather stepped beside her. "There was a fairy—an owl fairy, white with black striations. Your grandmother was terrified of her. Did you ever meet such a fairy?"

Not wanting to tell him the full truth, Elice shook her head.

He exhaled loudly. "Good. Good." He headed back to his chair, his shoulders rounded with weariness.

"Why?"

"She said things—terrible things. About the world ending and bringing about a new beginning. Your grandmother and I both made bargains with her. And the price . . ."

The ice castle began to tremble, a vibration that shook through Elice's bones. She held her breath until it passed. Then she asked, "What price?"

Her grandfather wouldn't look at her. He went to take a drink of water, only to find it frozen solid. Elice drew away the cold without even thinking. "Grandfather, what price?"

He heaved out a sigh. "I promised to save your grandmother, which I did."

"And what did Grandmother promise?"

He gently shook the cup, swirling his brown tea. It was already freezing again. "She promised she would give me a daughter. For the fairy's price, I lost my wife and my daughter." He threw the cup. Glass and ice shattered on Elice's fine floor.

The castle vibrated again. Beneath Elice's feet, the intricate fractals were split nearly in two. If it was this bad here, how much worse would it be closer to the destruction? She turned as a gale slammed into the room, hitting her with such force she had to duck and hold out her hand to shield her face. Thick layers of crystallized snow stirred up, forming dervishes. Beyond the snow, the sea whipped and chopped, the black waves growing higher and higher.

"I never met that fairy," Elice finally admitted. "But I think Adar did. Her name is Nagale. She's the one who helped Adar and Rycus learn about the Sundering. She and Chriel led Adar's ship here with the intention of kidnapping me."

Otec gasped. "By the Balance, she found you. Your mother banished her—took her ability to shift, clipped her wings, made her swear by the Balance to never have dealings with any in our family again. Yet still Nagale found a way to hurt you."

Elice turned to face him, blinking back tears. "But Grandfather, if what you say is true, why would she manipulate you and grandmother into having a child? What was the point?"

Before he could answer, the castle shook again, so hard that Elice pitched forward, barely getting her hands in front of her fast enough to break her fall. She landed on the broken bits of her grandfather's cup. Her palm throbbed, and she felt blood spreading out below her. Bits of ice rained down on her.

She lifted her hands. Winter surged through her, and an icy dome rose over her and her grandfather just as a chunk of the ceiling gave way. It slammed into the ice and gouged out a piece. Elice thickened the ice even as she scooted to where her grandfather had fallen, clutching his upper arm.

"Grandfather?" she cried over the sound of breaking ice. Just as quickly as it had begun, the shaking stopped. Elice yanked a sliver of glass from her palm and then gingerly touched her grandfather. "Your arm?"

Teeth clenched, he shook his head. "My collarbone," he gasped. "It's broken."

Everyone, fairy and human, was gone with her mother. Elice and her grandfather were completely alone in the queendom. The castle quaked, and she prepared herself to strengthen her icy shield, but the shaking subsided once more. "They have to be fighting again—it's the only explanation." And if the Balance was so broken that the ripples were this strong here, what were things like in Idara? In the clanlands?

"Stay here," Elice told her grandfather. Then she pulled a side of the ice dome back into winter and jumped over a jagged piece of ceiling that had shattered her pattern in the floor. She stepped onto her balcony and gasped, her hand flying to her mouth. The icy fields beyond the palace were gone, and chunks of her shattered forest now mixed with sea ice. Worst of all, the lower half of the palace was underwater. And the sea was steadily rising.

Calling from the well of power deep within her, Elice channeled the cold into the water, but instead of freezing, the palace's foundation cracked—a black rift that sped toward her balcony. She screamed and scrambled back.

The castle was built of ice. It would not hold against the sea. "Grandfather, we have to go—have to get up the mountain!"

Shoulder hunched and clutching his arm, he looked at her. "What's happening?"

Elice grasped his good arm and helped him to his feet. "The lower levels of the palace are underwater. I tried to freeze the sea, but that only made it worse."

She steered him toward her secret wall, the one that led to the caves. She pushed on the latch, but the pivot had broken, leaving the door leaning crookedly against the wall. "Elice, what are you doing?"

The castle shook again. Groaning in frustration, she slapped her hand against the secret door she'd spent months working on, drawing the ice through her and back to winter. Everything her hand touched disintegrated, revealing the corridor beyond, the one she'd built into the side of the palace so cleverly that no one had ever noticed it.

"You take after your grandmother," her grandfather said, and Elice thought she detected a hint of admiration. "Always seeing the details."

They hurried through the corridor just as another tremor hit, shaking them both so hard that Elice slammed into the wall and barely managed to hold onto her grandfather. Behind them, a huge chunk of ceiling shook loose. It crushed the floor as it fell, leaving a gaping hole that showed the churning black sea below. The floor beneath their feet spider-webbed, and suddenly Elice was falling.

Otec lunged for her, managing to grab her hair and hold on while she scrambled up, her scalp burning. They watched her bedroom crumble into the sea with a crash so deafening it obliterated all other sound. Her grandfather shoved her down the stairs. Elice turned back to see him motioning and shouting at her. Though she couldn't hear his words over the chaos, she knew he was trying to get her to leave him behind.

That was not going to happen.

She whirled around, then pulled winter through her and laid a slick layer of ice at their feet. They immediately lost their balance and shot downward. Elice could only hope they'd reach the cave before the palace completely crumbled.

Then a huge chunk of the passageway before them fell away. Elice concentrated, forming an ice bridge to cover the gap. They crossed open air and shot back into the tunnel. But it was too late. The tunnel completely collapsed around them. They were falling. Elice took hold of her grandfather's foot. She formed a pod of ice around them and thickened it even as she watched the sea rise toward them.

They slammed into the water. Elice pitched forward, smashing her face into the ice. The ocean swallowed them into its darkness. She closed her eyes to keep the scream in her throat. Their pod reeled as they shot toward the distant surface, and seconds later they burst back into the light.

Vision stained red with her own blood, Elice forced herself to pull her fists away from her ears and looked out over broken bits of the palace and forest churning around her and her grandfather. Another wave broke over them and shoved them under again. Something slammed into them from behind, sending them spinning and crushing one end of the pod. Sea water poured through but Elice quickly froze the hole shut.

She blinked blood from her eyes. "Grandfather, are you all right?"

He groaned in response. Before the ocean could toss them about some more, she set about freezing her grandfather and then herself to the sides of the pod. Next she shored up any cracks. The angry sea swallowed them and spit them out, over and over and over. It felt like an age had passed by the time the waves finally calmed.

Eyes clenched shut, Elice's grandfather lay against the ice, his face gray and his lips blue. She needed to get him to her cave, where she could work on his arm. She pulled in the ice above them and carefully stood to peer out. She couldn't see much of anything, but she was shocked at how warm it was outside— almost like summer. She stared at the horizon, searching for any sign of her home. But it was gone. They were alone.

"She must have won. Nelay must have won," Elice said softly, sorrow rising and falling inside her.

"No," her grandfather said, his voice thin. "If she had won, the winter fairies would have retreated to the safety of the queendom. Nelay would be hard pressed to touch the heart of winter, Winter Queen or no." He stopped, trying to catch his breath. "This is something else."

Elice knelt beside him and ripped off the hem of her dress to make a wrapping. She tried to take his arm, but he leaned away from her. "Leave it."

"I don't know where we are, Grandfather. I can't see any land." She tried to swallow her fear. They were adrift in thousands of leagues of sea. "If the Summer Queen didn't do this. . ." She faltered. "Then the only other answer is the Sundering."

He started to take a deep breath, but his chest hitched and he stiffened. "My girl." He finally opened his pale-blue eyes—the color of the winter sky.

Elice studied his gaze. "They wanted Mother. And when she was a woman, they took her as queen. But why? Why did they want her? She wasn't even born yet."

His brow furrowed and then he looked up at Elice. "It's you. Nagale wanted a child with the blood of Idara, the clanlands, and the highmen to overcome the old hatred. When your mother didn't stop the Sundering, Nagale put her hope in you."

"Why didn't they just tell us?"

"It's not in their nature." Her grandfather started shivering. But he couldn't possibly feel cold, for he was part of winter. "I'm fighting, and I'm losing. Oh, my girl, how can I leave you now?" He reached inside his overshirt and pulled out the beaver carving he had made so long ago. He pushed it into her hand with his icy fingers.

Elice attempted to draw the cold into her, but this cold wasn't from winter. It was something far more final. "Grandfather, I can't take this carving."

"Some lessons should be passed on." His hands fell back empty to rest on his chest. He strained toward her as if trying to speak. His body slowly relaxed, but his eyes remained fixed on hers. Just as he collapsed against the ice, he gasped, "Winter's heir." Then the light faded from his eyes, his gaze going unfocused.

"Grandfather?" Elice cried. "Grandfather?" She pressed her ear to his chest, but his heart had stilled.

16

E lice's weeping was interrupted by the sound of someone calling her name. She stood and peered over the edge of the ice pod. A huge owl flew toward her, followed by dozens and dozens of fairies. There was a spider fairy, a moss fairy, a bush fairy—with all white eyes—a brown owl fairy, and a snake fairy, which made Elice shudder. The wings of the lead fairy were white with black striations, and Elice knew this was the fairy who had orchestrated this whole thing.

It wasn't long before she realized the owl wasn't a fairy at all, but a winter owl. The creature riding its back was the fairy— an old one with knotted joints, skin like a withered old apple, and eyes that were gold under the rheum. Her few remaining feathers were tattered and looked brittle. The owl landed on the lip of the ice, and the fairy appraised Elice with a gaze sharp enough to cut.

"Fairies don't age." Elice couldn't think of anything else to say.

"I have been stripped of my right to shift and have therefore been trapped in this body for forty years." The old fairy smiled, revealing beaklike gums instead of teeth. "After all the trouble we have gone through to save the world, that's your question?"

Elice shrugged. "I know the rest. You arranged for my grandparents to marry and have my mother. And she had me. You want me to kill my own mother. I won't. Even if I could, I'm trapped here."

The fairy snapped her gums a few times. "Are you?"

Elice passed a hand down her face in frustration. "Why me? Adar is the warrior—go ask him."

The fairy dropped her gaze. "I doubt he will live through the night." The fairy's grip tightened around the owl's feathers. "The magic is failing. Breaking apart."

"Adar," Elice whispered, wishing desperately to go to him. She fought back the despair. "How? How do I stop this?"

The fairy gave a half smile. "Blood of the three kingdoms, but citizen of none. A daughter of winter and a lover of summer's son. Now you have everything to lose."

Elice felt the cold rippling from her. "Just tell me how."

The fairy leaned forward, giving Elice a view of her ruined wings. "The darkness comes."

"How?" Elice shouted.

The fairy smiled a terrible, cruel smile. "Your mother became the queen when you were within her womb. The same change wrought upon her was wrought upon you. Outshine the darkness."

"I don't have all her powers."

The fairy watched her. "Don't you?"

"I can't fly!"

"Can't you?"

Elice froze. Her grandfather had called her winter's heir.

"The quaking that destroyed the Winter Palace occurred when the queens faced off this evening," the fairy went on. "Nelay retreated, but they will clash again soon. The queens' powers are meant to balance one another—to complement each other. Using them against each other has set in motion the Sundering. If you don't channel the magic to save the world, it will destroy us all."

There wasn't room for anything but belief. Elice reached for the power deep within herself. She was a channel to winter, just like her mother. She focused on her back, concentrated the power of winter there. Imagined how it would feel to have wings. The cold gathered, tightening until it burned, and then there was a sweet release. Elice gasped in a breath and peered over her shoulder. Clear, prismatic wings flared from her back, sparking with an inner fire.

Her grandfather had been right. And if she was winter's heir because she was in her mother's womb when she changed, then Adar was summer's heir. Elice straightened to her full height, her wings spreading out to fill the horizon. She looked down at her grandfather, so still, and tucked the two halves of the beaver carving into her overdress. "I will remember what you taught me. I promise you."

She jumped a little, and a down stroke of her wings carried her upward. Hovering unsteadily, she drew the ice of the pod into herself. It disappeared. Her grandfather floated for a moment and then sank, his pale face vanishing beneath the dark waves.

Nagale and her owl flew up beside Elice. "Call up a southwest wind," instructed the fairy. "I'll show you the way."

"I don't need you to show me. I can feel her." Elice reached into winter, called for the wind, and stretched her wings. The wind rushed past her face and forced the tears from her eyes. The dark ocean slipped beneath her, turning slowly green-black and then navy.

Along the coast of Svass, the villages were flattened, their seagoing ships stranded far inland. Elice realized the sea had risen up, dragging the ships ashore and wiping out anything beyond her borders. She could only hope Sakari and her people were safe.

Elice flew fast, the wind shooting her across the sky like a falling star. Mountains rose up before her and increased in size and scope the farther she traveled. She passed the smoking ruins of a city. A smattering of survivors wandered, lost and dazed. There was a vibration in the air. The ground rumbled and birds exploded from the thick trees. A naked mountain thrust up from the land, black smoke bursting out in a thick cloud shaped like a mushroom.

"It's already begun," Nagale said from beside Elice.

Elice shifted midair, then diverted around the rising smoke to emerge on the other side. Above a high line of glacier-topped mountains, she saw her mother and Nelay wrapped around each other. Ice poured from her mother's hands, fire from Nelay's. As the elements met, the ground trembled again. A swath of trees shifted, then rolled down the mountainside, churning with rock and mud. The mass headed straight toward a village nestled beside a large lake.

Elice reached into winter and sent ice raging outward to create a barrier between the village and the slide. At that moment, she recognized the mountains—she'd been sculpting them all her life. This was Argonholm, the village of her father, where her grandmother still lived.

Just as that profound realization sank in, the rockslide blasted through the ice barrier. Screaming, the people tried to flee. Elice set her jaw. If she couldn't stop the rockslide, she would divert it. She formed an ice wedge just before the village. The slide tumbled into the ice and shifted to both sides, some spilling into the lake, some into a field. Even as Elice fed more ice into the wedge, a boulder bounced over it, collapsing a house as though it were made of sticks instead of rock and lumber. Rocks and debris spilled over the edge of the ice and toppled into the village.

And then it stopped. But the villagers couldn't stop running, for one of the mountains was spouting yellow and orange magma, along with the churning smoke. The queens' battle was tearing the world asunder.

Elice dove toward the battling queens and formed a jagged-edged wall of ice between them. The queens reeled back from each other, their eyes snapping to Elice. "Stop!" she shouted. "Can't you see you're destroying the whole world?"

Ilyenna gaped at her. "Elice—you have wings! What happened?"

Keeping a strong barrier between the Summer and Winter Queens, Elice carefully watched them both. "You have to stop this, Mother. Stop this war, before the world is gone forever."

"How is this possible?" Nelay asked, the fire fading from her eyes.

Studying the woman who loved Adar, Elice found she could not hate her. No matter how much damage she had caused. "I am winter's heir, as Adar is summer's."

"Adar is dying." Nelay's voice broke. "He may already be gone."

A chasm opened up in Elice's chest. "You can save him!"

Disbelief and hope mingled on Nelay's face. But before she could choose either emotion, fire erupted beneath them, and a churning cloud of ash and magma exploded. Elice only had time for one powerful down stroke before the smoke enveloped her.

"Elice!" her mother cried.

Holding her breath, Elice whipped around, eyes burning as she tried to catch sight of anything. But it was dark. So dark. The old fear rose up inside her. She had to get out of the smoke, get to the light. She pumped her wings. Static crackled through the air, lifting the hairs on her body. Heat boiled up from below. She tried to shift her magic, to shield herself from the fire and ash rising toward her.

With a deafening boom, magma burned through her thick ice like it was nothing. She screamed as it splattered her feet, and then she gasped in a ragged breath of poisonous fumes. She was choking. Falling. Then something slammed into her. Arms wrapped around her and dragged her through the air. The heat no longer blistered her skin, though the smoke still choked her.

It was growing lighter, a thick charcoal instead of the awful black. Elice coughed, her throat raw. The Summer Queen had saved her. A few more pumps of Nelay's wings, and she set Elice down in the shelter of a rock outcropping at the base of the mountain.

"How can I save him?" Nelay asked her.

Elice looked up through tears. "He is your heir," she gasped between coughs. "He's had the power all along. Same as me. Give him the realm—name him your king. Then summer will embrace him and heal his hurts, as it healed my mother's long ago."

Nelay shot to the sky without hesitation, her form almost immediately swallowed up by smoke. Then she was gone, and Elice was left in the choking vapors and falling ash. She tried to stand, hoping to glide down to the valley that had to be somewhere below, but pain stabbed up from her feet. She didn't dare look at them to assess the damage.

With every poisonous breath she took, her head grew lighter and her wings more limp. Then a strong wind pumped beside her and she was enveloped by her mother's cool arms and carried from the churning blackness of the lava cloud. Elice gasped a breath of clean air into her charred lungs. Bits of cooling magma fell from what was left of her feet. Her mother settled on the far side of a gentle rise, where they collapsed, Ilyenna's wings trailing behind her like murdered ghosts. She leaned over her daughter.

Elice couldn't seem to catch her breath. Breathing hurt terribly. Much worse than her feet, which she still couldn't bring herself to look at. But if the look of horror on her mother's face was any indication, it was very bad. Curled on her side, Elice saw that she lay in a field of grass and dandelions. She reached out and grazed her fingertips across the soft, spiny petals. Then she gave into the great, hacking coughs. She spit black mucous into the grass, then vomited. Her mother pounded her back, her face lined with dread.

Head spinning, Elice lay back on the grass and stared at the churning column of smoke that blotted out the sky. Dozens of bolts of lightning continuously sparked in the darkness. She felt strangely disconnected, like she was watching all of this from far away.

"Elice, you're turning blue. You have to breathe. Take it in."

Her gaze shifted from the smoke and lightning to her mother leaning over her. "Where are we?"

Her mother's eyes glistened. "The Shyle. We're home."

Elice smiled a little. "I saved Argonholm . . . from a rockslide." She choked and gasped. "They wanted me to kill you," she admitted. "Tricked me into bargaining them for it." She tried to laugh but ended up coughing instead. "I showed them. I beat their bargains." Her life would be the price, not her mother's.

"Of course you would never murder me. You're my daughter." Her mother formed ice crystals over Elice's skin and scrubbed the soot from her face.

Wheezing, Elice watched her mother go through the motions of healing—motions that by all accounts had once been second nature to Ilyenna, but now seemed foreign and awkward. "I'm sorry I hurt you, Mother. I love you."

Ilyenna rested a hand on Elice's check. "I know."

Elice relaxed into the field, one hand still grasping a dandelion. She could feel her life slipping away, like water through her fingers. "You could save me. Name me your heir and stop the Sundering."

Ilyenna's mouth tightened. "There are worse things than death, Elice. I know I should love you. And yet, I don't. My love for you is trapped beneath a layer of ice and I cannot reach it. So

I must do what I have always done—what your father would have wanted me to do. It broke me, becoming a queen. It broke me, and I will not let it break you."

Elice tried to touch her mother's face, but her arm was too heavy and it fell back to her side. "It won't break me, Mother, because I am your heir. I was born with the magic of winter."

Ilyenna looked at Elice, her face strangely composed. "No, my daughter. Go to your father. Go to your rest. I will not leave you in this broken world."

Elice felt oddly at peace. Her mother was capable of acting out of love, but not really feeling it. Elice forgave her for that. Forgave her for failing to stop the Sundering. Forgave her for not loving her in the gentle way a mother should. Giving Elice her grandfather had been the best Ilyenna could do with what little humanity she could remember.

Elice felt herself sinking into the loam beneath her and rising up to the sky at the same time. She was everywhere and nowhere and everything and nothing. Then her father was there, his face smiling at her. She smiled back, ready to go with him and leave her broken body behind.

But he shook his head sadly. "The price has not been paid, Elice. First you must destroy the Winter Queen." Then his ghost knelt beside her and whispered a phrase. He gave her a gentle smile, stood, and pulled back into the vapors.

Elice felt herself rising up, following him, but the phrase he'd given her left her lips moments before her body stilled. "You still have the same soul."

Ilyenna gasped. "Rone?" She choked on a sob as tears ran slick down her face. Then she leaned forward, blocking Elice's view of the world beyond, and pressed her cold lips to Elice's. All the scattered parts of Elice suddenly slammed back together with crystal clarity. Her body healed in an instant. A connection to the fairies snapped into place. Ice and snow and storm converged through her, whipping with enough force to freeze her soul and shatter it to a thousand pieces.

But Elice was impervious to the cold.

She gasped in a breath, filling her lungs with clean, cold air. Every remaining fairy turned and locked their eyes on her. The trembling of the earth stilled and the volcanoes ceased spewing smoke and ash and fire. Elice pushed herself to her feet, feeling at once whole and perfect in a way she had never felt before. Her wings yawed out behind her. She stretched out a winter wind to clear away some of the smoke.

She took another free breath, her lungs no longer aching, and turned to find her mother crumpled on the ground, tears streaming down her face as she stared at Elice. The wings at Ilyenna's back slowly faded before disappearing altogether. The hard, sharp-edged aura that always surrounded her softened, like snow melting and life springing back. Her cutting expression thawed until she looked like a young girl, shivering with cold.

"I'm—I'm so sorry. I . . . oh, Elice!"

Her mother launched herself to her feet and threw herself into her daughter's arms. Her body was soft and yielding and wracked by sobs. Elice was so shocked by her mother's sudden display of emotion, she could only stand frozen for a moment. Then she relaxed and wrapped her arms around her mother.

Ilyenna was shivering hard, so Elice did what she'd done a thousand times for Adar—she drew the cold back into winter. Her mother stopped shivering and laid her head on her daughter's shoulder. "You saved me, Elice. All those years of the best parts of me trapped beneath the ice, and all the horrible things I said and did, what I failed to do, yet you never stopped searching for the light within me."

Tears streamed down Elice's face. The hurt and the neglect and the loneliness faded a little. She knew it would take time, but they had a lifetime to make up for what they had lost.

Ilyenna pulled back a little. "Where's your grandfather?"

Fresh tears spilled down Elice's cheeks. She reached into her pocket and pulled out the two halves of the beaver. Her mother seemed to understand.

"How will he ever know how sorry I am?" Ilyenna asked.

"I saw my father. He told me to tell you that you have the same soul. And wherever my Father is, Grandfather is there with him. My grandmother, too. Someday we'll see them again." Elice had never been surer of anything in her life.

17

The ground rocked beneath Elice. Behind her, a massive explosion of magma and fire tore through the sky. She whirled around as lightning flashed. "But the war is over. The Sundering should be over!"

She didn't have time to dwell on it. Another explosion rocked the mountain, sending a slide of magma toward them. Elice wrapped her mother in her arms and pumped hard to glide down the mountain just ahead of an ash cloud. In the field before the village, Elice set her down.

"I don't understand," Ilyenna cried.

Elice studied the cloud, the fires the magma had started. "The Balance is still distorted. Something is preventing it from righting itself." What if Nelay hadn't reached Adar in time? What if it hadn't worked?

"Mother, I have to go."

Ilyenna gripped her hands. "Find him."

Elice formed a dome of ice so thick she could barely see past it, and then she sealed it to winter to protect Shyleholm and her mother from the magma. She could only hope it would be enough. Then Elice shot to the sky and headed south, winter wind propelling her forward at tremendous speed. But not so fast that she missed the volcanoes spewing ash and magma, the smoke choking the air, the sea surging past its boundaries, wiping out everything in its path. Rivers diverting from their natural course to plough through villages.

Everything was in commotion and upheaval. Everything was shattering and breaking. Suddenly a hot desert wind that smelled of growing things and fire collided with Elice's cold winter wind. Black storm clouds spread across the sky. Lightning raced across the heavens.

What if Adar was already dead and this was Nelay's rage? What if the Summer Queen blamed Elice and came after her and the war began anew? The world wouldn't survive. She knew it wouldn't.

Then, through the darkness of cloud and ash, a brilliant beam of light shot across the horizon, so bright Elice had to pull up and shield her eyes. At first, she thought it was a flash of lightning. Only it didn't fade away, but grew brighter. Blinking against the brilliance, she realized the light was in the shape of wings.

"Adar?" Elice whispered. She pumped her wings hard, watching his face come into sight. Her eyes drank him in—his midnight eyes and tattooed scalp. Then his wings, exuding light with each down stroke.

She flared her wings and threw herself back to slow down at the same moment he did. And then they were in each other's arms. Heat poured off him, mixing with the cold that radiated from her and creating a vortex that twisted around them, churning hair and clothing, and sending scattered rainbows in all directions.

Thunder cracked and the rain sheeted down, washing away layers of ash and soot and clearing the air. As two pairs of wings kept them aloft, Elice pulled back to look at Adar's face to make sure it was really him. That he was really alive. He took her neck in his hands and kissed her like he'd found something he thought he'd lost forever. Between them, her pendant of fire and ice flickered blue.

She was sobbing with joy. "You're alive!"

Adar took her face in his hands, his expression anguished as he wiped the rain from her cheeks. "Did you kill her? Did you kill your mother?"

Elice smiled up at him. "No. I didn't have to. She named me her heir and gave me her powers."

He gazed at her in wonder. "How did you know that was possible for either of us?"

"I think my grandfather figured it out first. He called me winter's heir, and then the fairies asked me why I would have some of my mother's powers and not others. As soon as I made my own wings appear, I knew."

Adar's gaze had caught on something in the distance. "Look."

She followed his eyes and saw that the volcanoes were no longer belching smoke and magma. The earth and sea were still and calm. The rain had cleared the air and extinguished the fires. Elice looked past him at Thanjavar in the distance. The city appeared to be mostly intact.

Adar let out a long breath and rested his forehead against hers, brushing the tears off her cheeks with his thumbs. "I think the Sundering is over."

"Yes. But not the rebirth," said a voice. Elice and Adar turned to see Nagale regarding them from atop her owl. A thousand winter and summer fairies hovered behind her. "Come with me."

She led Elice and Adar back to the fields around Shyleholm. A huge lava flow had cut down the mountainside, carving a path through the forest before coming dangerously close to the ice bubble. Elice set down beside the steaming mass and forced a wave of cold to harden it. It crumbled into large chunks that shone like black glass. When she was sure it was safe, she dissolved the ice dome, pulling it back into herself.

Ilyenna waited on the other side. She took one look at Adar and turned her attention to the fairy. "This was your plan all along, wasn't it? That our children would fall in love."

The rush of a thousand oncoming wings filled the air. Elice turned toward the sound and watched as another group of fairies approached, carrying a person in their nets. Elice recognized their passenger moments before the fairies set her down.

As Nelay detangled herself from the nets, Nagale eyed the former queen. "And you think you are the most brilliant strategist to have ever lived. I have been planning this moment for eighty years. The Sundering is complete. A new age has begun, different than the one before."

Ilyenna took a few steps forward to face the aged fairy. "I know you—I banished you."

Nagale gave a rueful smile. "And you are no longer queen." She turned her gaze back to Elice and Adar. "The magic must change. Choose."

Elice didn't understand.

Nelay came to stand beside her son. "Choose what?"

Nagale gestured to the fairies around her. "The rules that will bind the new magic and give it form."

Elice shared a look with Adar and the two former queens.

"But that would destroy you," Nelay said.

Nagale stretched out her ruined wings. "We cannot be destroyed. The rules made us into this form. The rules will give us our new form."

The fairies hovered silently, their faces void of expression. More came, hundreds of thousands of them, winter and summer fairies alike. Elice turned in a circle, taking in the multitude of fairies—ice, snake, lion, tree, frog, insect. She need only look into their grave eyes to understand this was the end of them.

They knew it, but they were not afraid. In fact, they almost seemed relieved.

But Elice was afraid. "Will I lose my magic too?"

"That depends on what you choose." Nagale gestured to the fairies around her. "We cannot be destroyed. We are the magic, and we tire of this form. Now choose."

"But what if I choose wrong?" Elice asked in a whisper.

"All magic contains both light and dark. The Balance will see that your form does, too."

When you chose the good, you also chose the evil. Chriel's words flashed through Elice's mind. Knowing she couldn't do this alone, she shot a look at her mother. "We all choose. Beginning with you, Mother."

Ilyenna took a deep breath and let it out slowly. "No single being should control the magic—it is too much power. It should be spread out among many people."

Elice nodded and turned to Adar. "The magic shouldn't control the seasons," he said. "It's too easy for a corrupt individual to cause harm." He glanced at Ilyenna.

Elice looked to Nelay, who studied the ground. "No more fairies," said the former Summer Queen. "Give the magic back to the creatures and let them control themselves. But allow mankind to keep a bit of it, so that we are not powerless against whatever form the new magic takes."

Nagale turned her attention to Elice. "And what would you choose, my queen?"

Elice studied the decrepit fairy, wishing Chriel were here instead. "I would ask for your advice, for you have seen one age end and another begin once before, and I have not."

The fairy nodded in approval. "There must always be a price, child. Choose the price, choose the magic."

Elice thought about it for a long time and then lifted her head. *Outshine the darkness.* "Mankind can only use magic to fight evil."

The fairy took a long, slow breath and let it out. "So it shall be. Let magic take its new form."

Even as Elice watched, Nagale's body seemed to be softening. She gave a great shudder and then her entire body was covered in pristine feathers of white and black. The spark of intelligence didn't fade from Nagale's eyes as she met Elice's gaze. All around them, fairies turned into their animals. Snow fairies shifted to flakes. Ice fairies to ice. Frost fairies to frost. Some of the animals' eyes still held far too much intelligence, but something was missing—that otherworldly aura that trailed a finger of warning down a human spine.

The animals crept and slunk and slithered away. Birds took flight. But the owl remained, her gaze locked on the magma flow. At a sharp cracking sound, Elice whipped around. A perfectly circular rock, nearly the size of her chest, had broken from the flow to land with a thud. As she watched, another popped free, leaving two craters behind. They were black like the rest, but strange, as if they sucked in light and turned it to shadow. The more Elice looked, the more the darkness seemed to consume her.

She gave a gasp and faced the fairy. "What is it?" she asked, but the owl was already gone.

Nelay took a few steps forward and crouched before the round rock. "I've never seen its like before in all of the Summer Realm."

Adar reached down to lift it, the muscles of his arms straining. His brow furrowed. "It's hot, like it just came from the fire."

Elice didn't know what to make of this—didn't know what form this new magic would take. She looked behind her to make sure her prismatic wings were still tucked behind her back. Then she reached for winter and felt it just as strong as she had before. "I don't feel any different, do you?" she asked Adar.

His various colors of flames danced in quick succession across his palm. "Just as amazing as I've always been."

Ilyenna hadn't looked away from the large, circular rock. "Can you break it?" she asked.

Adar held out his hand for her battle axe. Ilyenna handed it to him without another word. He swung it down onto the rock. The sound rang out, but there wasn't so much as a scratch on the stone.

Elice backed away, hoping whatever she'd created wasn't as bad as the fairies had been. She glanced up to see her mother already halfway out of sight as she trekked down the slope. "Where are you going?"

Her mother pointed down the hill, toward the village nestled in the arms of the mountains. "I have family down there. *We* have family down there, and I haven't seen them in decades."

Elice's breath caught in her throat at a sudden memory of warm sunlight on her face and the smell of crushed grass. She was finally in Shyleholm, the village of her mother and grandfather for as far back as memory.

"I think we finally made it home." She reached out to take Adar's hand.

He looked back at Nelay. "Mother, you don't have to come."

She let out a long sigh. "I think it's time Ilyenna and I became allies." She gave Elice a smile, then moved forward and pressed a kiss to her cheek. Adar hugged his mother and then Nelay hurried after Ilyenna.

Elice made to follow them, but Adar took her hand in his. She squinted up at him, the brilliance of his wings making her eyes water. "Elly—I can call you that now, right?"

She smiled and stepped back into his arms. "Only if you marry me."

He grinned. "All right, but I get to do the cooking. No offense, but you're terrible."

She cocked an eyebrow. "And to think, I almost let you drown."

He pulled her into his arms and wrapped his wings around her, his lips claiming hers. She claimed him right back. Light and color spilled across the valley. Though the wind held the bite of winter, the sun was warm and bright.

Epilogue

N ew grass sprouted over the scorch marks left by the volcano. Then a little sapling grew. Every summer its boughs stretched to fill the sky, and each winter it bowed under a heavy mantle of snow. A large home was built on the rise a short distance from the tree. A man and a woman lived there with their six children—three with the powers of winter, and three with the powers of summer. The woman would often stand under the shade of the still-growing tree and watch the stones with a breathless wariness, as if she knew something evil would come of them and was determined to stop it.

One summer, a boy even burned the name of a village girl in the tree's bark with his smoking finger. The years passed and the children married and had children of their own. Those children had more children. With each generation, the magic seemed to splinter until each child was born with only one power. For the winter children—the bite of frost, the colors of the aurora, or the calling of the blizzard. For the summer children—the nimbus of the blue fire, the heat of the white, or the growling of a thunderstorm.

Some even controlled the wind.

Still the couple lived on. They would come out sometimes and stare at the rocks, now partially obscured by soil and growing grasses, though the snow never seemed to touch them. Until one day, long after their grandchildren's grandchildren had passed on, the woman and man died.

They were buried by their progeny under the great boughs of the tree, which spread roots out to curl around them like the old friends they were. But with the couple's death died their vigilance.

Hundreds of years had passed. Temples were built, and wars again touched the sheltered valley. The great tree grew brittle and creaked with the wind. It was then that the lightning storm came. Flames licked up the tree's rough bark, as the flames from the volcano had done to its forbearer. Pinecones crackled and popped, and the air filled with the smell of burning. The monstrous tree fell, landing on a pair of strangely formed rocks. The tree burned bright and hot, its life wood crumbling to coals.

When the fire had moved on and only ashes and trails of weak smoke remained, the wind picked up, blowing gray ash in little dervishes across the blackened landscape. That wind blew away the ashes of the great tree, revealing two perfectly round stones.

But though the fire was gone, the stones glowed an evil red that shifted like the beat of a heart. Then one rock cracked and an angular piece fell off. A great yellow eye, slitted and rimmed with spikes, peered out at the beautiful destruction all around it. From deep inside the egg, a dragon smiled.

THE END

To receive Amber Argyle's starter library for free,
join her spam-free newsletter (http://eepurl.com/l8fl1).

AUTHOR'S NOTE

In *Winter Queen*, I explored the theme "Strong as stone, supple as a sapling"—that to be strong, sometimes you have to bend or risk breaking.

In *Summer Queen*, I explored the theme "To rise from the ashes, first you must burn." Everyone crashes, everyone burns. Everyone fails. It's what you do after failing that's important. When you pick yourself up, learn from your failures, and move on to something better.

In *Daughter of Winter* and *Winter's Heir*, the theme is "outshine the darkness." Everyone has moments when they falter. When hope seems lost. When life shatters around them. But the hero always stands up. Even in the midst of hopelessness and despair. The hero always tries one more time.

And that's why I love fiction. That's why I love heroes. Because we all have those moments. When the night is at its darkest and there is no hope of living till the dawn. But you just keep trying. Because giving up is not in your nature. Or maybe because there's nothing left to do but keep trying. You dig deep and pull upon courage you didn't know you had. And you triumph.

I hope my fiction has given you that kind of hope. I pray that my words have touched you. Uplifted you. That in some small way, the courage of my characters will remind you of your own courage. That even if the very jaws of hell gape after you, you can find it within yourself to keep trying.

Even if it's for just one more second.

And then the second after that.
And the second after that.

ACKNOWLEDGEMENTS

U pon preparing my tenth acknowledgments page, I've realized that I've run out of clever witticisms. Henceforth, I shall proceed with making stuff up.

Thanks go out to my curling team: the skip (she who tells everyone what to do, with very little spittle), Charity West; the lead sweep (she who throws stones and rarely ever hits anyone), Linda Prince; the second (she who excels at knocking out other people's stones), Lara Sava; the third (she who shall not *not* be named), Michelle Argyle; the fourth (he who eats popcorn), Robert Defendi; the fifth (she who makes the popcorn), Julie Titus; and the sixth (she who cleans up the mess), Cathy Nielson.

Thanks to the maintenance crew: Derek Smith (he who drives the Zamboni), Corbin Smith (he who gets kicked out of games for booing cheerleaders); Connor Smith (he who peed on the ice), and Lily Smith (she who bedazzled our stones). Thanks go to God, without whom we would have no one to dedicate our opening prayers to.

We have a shot at the gold at this year's Olympics. Or at least Honorable Mention at the city leagues. As soon as we find a city league. We may have to drive to Canada. And under no circumstances will Bob be allowed to drive

Amber Argyle is the number-one bestselling author of the Witch Song Series and the Fairy Queen Series. Her books have been nominated for and won awards and have been translated into French and Indonesian.

Amber graduated cum laude from Utah State University with a degree in English and physical education, a husband, and a two-year-old. Since then, she and her husband have added two more children, which they are actively trying to transform from crazy small people into less crazy larger people.

To receive Amber Argyle's starter library for free, simply tell her where to send it (http://eepurl.com/l8fl1).